Murder Clause

BOOKS BY RAEGAN TELLER

Murder in Madden

The Last Sale

Secrets Never Told

The Fifth Stone

Time to Prey

Murder Clause

MURDER CLAUSE

Raegan Teller

Pondhawk Press LLC

Columbia, South Carolina

Pondhawk Press LLC
PO Box 290033
Columbia, SC 29229

Publisher's Note: This is a work of fiction. Names, characters, places, and incidents are a product of the author's imagination. Locales and public names are sometimes used for atmospheric purposes. Any resemblance to actual people, living or dead, or to businesses, companies, events, institutions, or locales is completely coincidental.

ISBN 979-8-9880730-0-0

Dedicated to Irene Stern,
a dear friend and my partner in crime

"The two most important days of your life are the day you
were born and the day you find out why."

Mark Twain

PREFACE

For more than a year, I've been working on this book, which has gone through numerous drafts and iterations. Its working title during that time was *Epilogue*, as it was meant to be the conclusion of what happened to Enid and Josh after they left Madden to start a life together. But as I delved deeper into the narrative, I realized the questions that haunted my thoughts would ultimately shape the story.

The Enid Blackwell Mystery Series has always been about more than just solving crimes. It's about the journey of a woman trying to find her place in the world, grappling with her past and present, and trying to make sense of it all.

In *Murder Clause*, Enid is faced with some of her most profound questions yet. What does it mean to live a purposeful life? Can we recognize our purpose when we're living it, or do we only see it in hindsight? And what happens when we suppress that purpose, when we ignore the calling that's inside us?

As always, Enid is driven by the quest for truth. But in this story, she must confront a truth closer to home: her own purpose and the consequences of ignoring it. And along the way, she'll discover whether love can truly transcend the void left by unfulfilled aspirations.

Thank you for joining me and Enid on this journey. I hope her story will inspire you to ask your own questions about your truth. And most of all, I hope you'll enjoy the mystery and intrigue that lies ahead.

Raegan Teller

CHAPTER 1

Roo pulled into a parking space in front of the coffee shop and bookstore, one of a dozen small businesses along Blakeley's main street. As usual, the fire-engine red, 1967 Chevy step-side pickup got admiring and curious stares. She'd gotten used to the attention it created, and while she didn't like it, the truck had belonged to her late father. Of course, when she had to do stakeouts or surveillance work, she rented a more inconspicuous car.

She had been up until late last night researching the town's namesake, Miller Blakeley. One article referred to him as "Hemi," his college nickname inspired by Ernest Hemingway. Roo found that interesting because her own nickname was inspired by a literary character: a young kangaroo in the Winnie the Poo series. Roo's mother couldn't decide between Ruby or Grace, so she settled on Ruby-Grace as the first name. During elementary school, Roo's friends shortened it, and the moniker stuck.

Walking into the shop was like stepping back decades in time. The wide, worn floorboards creaked when Roo walked to the back of the room to investigate the shelves of books across the wall.

"Roo, it can't be. Is that you?"

Roo turned around quickly to face the voice. "Enid? Oh, my God. I heard you had moved somewhere down this way."

Enid Blackwell came from behind the counter to hug Roo. "Yep, I live here." She gestured around the shop. "And this is my little piece of paradise. You know I've always loved bookstores that were also coffee shops, so we bought this one when we moved here."

"I also heard you had married that gorgeous man you were dating."

Enid held up her hand, showing a wedding band of diamonds and turquoise stones custom designed by a Santa Fe jeweler. "Josh and I have been married almost two years now. And what about you?"

"Look at you, Mrs. Josh Hart. You're grinning like a Cheshire cat. Me? I'm still doing freelance insurance investigations."

"I was sorry to hear about your Aunt Catherine."

"Yes, sadly she died of Covid last year."

Enid took Roo's hand in hers. "She was a good woman and a wonderful historian for Madden. She did a great job preserving the town's history and its stories."

"One of the last things she said to me was how thankful she was that she got those extra years of living because you helped rescue her from that horrible place where she had been held captive."

"That was a sad situation. I'm just glad we were able to find her and get her out." Enid gestured toward the slightly worn velvet chairs. "Have a seat, and I'll bring you something. What kind of coffee would you like?"

"Just plain ol' coffee. Do you have time to sit with me for a few minutes? I could use your help."

"Of course. I'll bring us some coffee and be right there."

Roo browsed the bookshelves until Enid returned with a tray of steaming cups and two walnut brownies.

"Wait, did you make those brownies? When I stayed with you, you couldn't boil a pot of water without burning it."

Enid laughed. "Was I that bad?" She handed a cup to Roo.

"Yes, you were." Roo took a bite of brownie. "OMG! These are great. Now I know you didn't make them."

"Okay, I confess. The previous owner of the shop sold just coffee, tea and desserts. She loves to bake, so she agreed to supply all the sweets we sell. I added the books when we bought it." Enid toyed with her wedding band, appearing to be lost in thought. "But I am learning to cook."

A customer walked into the shop. "I'll be right there," Enid said. "Can you come to dinner tonight?" she asked Roo. "We can talk then. And you're welcome to stay in our guest room, such as it is. We have an apartment upstairs. It's small but convenient. My commute to work is those stairs," she said pointing.

"Are you sure? I don't want to intrude."

"Josh would love to see you again." But let me help this customer first.

· · ·

Five hours later, Roo, Enid, and Josh were sitting at the dinner table finishing off their meal with coffee. "I'm still in shock," Roo said. "First I find out you're living in Blakeley, you own a coffee and book shop, and you've learned to cook." Roo threw her hands in the air, as she often did when excited. "Dinner was DE-licious. I mean it." She pointed to Enid's cup. "And now you're drinking coffee. You were a diehard tea drinker. What's happening in the universe?"

"Obviously, she married the perfect man to change her," Josh said, smiling.

"Yeah, okay. I have to admit, you both look amazingly happy." She sighed. "And I'm still investigating fraudulent life insurance claims, have no man, and have only enough savings to squeak by. What's wrong with this picture?"

"Enid said you wanted to talk to her, so I'm going to let you two go to the living room, and I'll clean up the table," Josh said.

Roo threw her hands in the air again. "Now I find out you have a husband that will do the dishes. It's just too perfect."

Josh began collecting the silverware. "Not really. I'm sure you'll get the real scoop on me from Enid."

"Thanks for doing the dishes, babe," Enid said to Josh. She turned to Roo. "Let's take him up on that offer and go to the living room."

"I'll get my notes and be there shortly."

When Roo returned, she sat in a chair across from Enid. "Are you sure you don't mind me running this case past you? You were a great investigative journalist, and I could use your insights. But I don't want to intrude on your new life."

"Of course you're not intruding. I'm so happy to see you and I'll help any way I can. Tell me about your case."

Roo leaned back in her chair. "I'm not sure why I thought I needed my notes. I know every little detail of this case by heart. I'll try to sum it up as quickly as I can. You're living here, so you obviously know the Blakeley family."

"Not personally, but I certainly know about Miller Blakeley and how his great-grandfather started this town. Everyone here knows the history and who he is."

"While I was doing research, I read that the town was originally set up as a writers' colony. That's so cool. But is it true?"

"Yes, Blakeley gathered a group of his writer friends and together they bought a parcel of land, which at the time was in the middle of nowhere. Franklin Blakeley, the great-grandfather, wanted to create a Shangri-La, a small paradise for writers."

"So what happened?"

"Like all fantasies, Blakeley became a victim of reality. Most of the writers' children grew up and moved away and many of the writers eventually moved away too. Or died. The town was drying up, so Blakeley invited a few businesses to move in, and over time Blakeley became just another small town. It's an artsy kind of place though. We still have a lot of writers and artists who live here."

"Ah, yes, reality sucks sometimes. I can see why you wanted to come here, but what about Josh? Surely he's not content being the police chief of this little place. No offense toward your town, but just say'n."

"Josh is their part-time chief. The town can't afford a full-time police chief, nor do they need one. There's virtually no crime here."

"So Josh just teaches you to cook, cleans off the table, and caters to your every whim?"

Enid shifted her weight on the sofa. "He's also doing some contract work for the state." Enid smiled and pointed to Roo's notes. "Why don't we get back to your case."

"Oh, all right. So you obviously know about Guinette Blakeley's death. I mean, how can you not know about it, right?"

Enid nodded. "The whole town was shocked when we heard she had committed suicide. So sad."

"As I understand it, she was loved by everyone, gave to charities—the whole small-town, Southern belle thing." Roo pointed to a manila folder in her lap. "That's why I'm here, to investigate her death. If it was suicide, I'll recommend to the insurance company that they pay her husband. He was the sole beneficiary."

"I didn't think the insurance company would pay if it was suicide."

"Her policy had a clause that excluded coverage for death by suicide for the first two years of the policy. Her policy was taken out a little more than two years ago."

"Her husband appears to be devastated," Enid said.

Roo's right eyebrow lifted. "Really?"

"What's that look about?"

"I'm just investigating at this point. Not ready to draw any conclusions. Or at least none I can prove." Roo paused. "The insurance company is pressuring me to close it out. They're obviously anxious to pay a prominent policyholder and move on."

"And you?"

"I'd love another one of those brownies if you have one."

CHAPTER 2

Enid returned from the kitchen with two more brownies and fresh cups of coffee. "So you obviously have some doubts or questions about what happened."

"Just like you have a nose for a news story, I have a nose for . . . well, let's just say inconsistencies," Roo said. "The Blakeleys are in serious debt. Miller made some bad investments and then got himself hooked on Oxi."

"You mean oxycodone?"

Roo nodded. "An addict can take up to 80 milligrams a day. The pills can cost up to $80 each. That's close to $30,000 a year."

"That's a lot of money, but I imagine he can afford it."

"Well, then there are the gambling debts."

"I knew he went to Vegas a few times a year."

"And he plays a lot of online poker, according to my sources."

Enid sat back in her chair. "So are you actually thinking Miller may have killed his wife for the insurance money?"

Roo shrugged. "There are five million reasons he might have, plus another ten million in her estate."

Josh walked into the room. "Anything you ladies need?"

When Roo jumped up and hugged him, he appeared stunned. "What did I do to deserve that?" he asked.

"That's a thank-you for marrying and taking care of my favorite red-headed friend. You're lucky to have each other. I'm insanely envious, of course." Roo patted her stomach.

"I'm full. The brownies and coffee were delicious."

When Josh left the room, Roo leaned forward and whispered. "Will you help me?"

"I'm not sure what I can do. I'm not a reporter any longer and if I start asking too many questions, the locals will get suspicious. Some of these families have lived here for generations, and it's a cliquish community. They tend to be suspicious of any outsiders."

"Do you have a local newspaper?"

Enid laughed. "No, I'm afraid not."

"Maybe you can just casually ask around for me. Anything you can find out might help. And I'll continue my investigation." She paused. "Here's the problem, though. The insurance company wants to close this file, so if I don't find something concrete soon, they'll pay Miller Blakeley."

Enid leaned her head back against the sofa. "Josh wouldn't be happy if I got involved in local matters or gossip. He's trying to blend in and keep a low profile."

"Come on. He's got to know you're bored. I mean, no offense, but you're too young to retire to this sleepy little place, charming as it may be."

"I'm trying to build a new life here. It's not easy at times, and I'm definitely having to adjust. But I love having the shop. Just remember, I have to live here when you pack up and go home. My store sales could suffer if I upset the citizens."

Roo threw up her hands. "Okay, I get it. Sorry I asked."

"Don't be mad. I'd like to help you, but we're really trying to blend in here."

Roo jumped up. "Never thought I'd see the day Enid

Blackwell walked away from finding the truth. But I get it."

. . .

Later that night when Josh and Enid were sitting in bed reading, Enid told him about her conversation with Roo and her request for Enid to snoop around.

Josh threw his book onto the bed. "Absolutely not. You know we can't draw unnecessary attention to ourselves here."

Enid sighed. "That what I told her. But I wanted you to know why she's here."

Josh pulled Enid to him and put his arm around her. "Sorry. I didn't mean to sound off like that. The coroner said Guinette's death was suicide, and I have no reason to believe otherwise." He pulled her closer. "Are you happy? I mean here, in Blakeley?"

"I'm happy anywhere you are."

Grinning, Josh stroked her hair. "Right answer. But you know what I mean."

"When we came here, we agreed we'd stay until your assignment is over. Then we can decide what happens next." She squeezed his hand. "Sometimes I think we're destined to be nomads, constantly wandering from place to place. But for now, I enjoy running the shop."

"Just promise me one thing, because I know that no matter what I say, you're going to get involved. Just don't do anything to cause Blakeley's citizens to be suspicious of us. We've got to blend in as much as possible. Remember, we don't know how much longer we'll be here."

Enid kissed his chest, the hairs tickling her nose. "I promise."

CHAPTER 3

After breakfast of scones and coffee with Enid, Roo told Enid she'd be back later that evening. Roo was disappointed Enid hadn't agreed to help her. It wasn't that Roo needed the help as much as she would like to have worked with her friend again. But Josh and Enid seemed so happy together, and Roo didn't want to cause any friction between them. Besides, she hadn't known Enid was in Blakeley before she came here, so nothing was lost.

Roo's first stop was to see the local insurance agent who had sold the policy on Guinette to Miller Blakeley. The independent agent sold mostly life insurance policies for several companies, including the one that hired Roo to investigate the suicide.

The agency was a few doors down, so she could easily walk. She started to check the meter where her truck was parked but then realized there were none. Easy parking on the street, with no meters, was definitely a perk of small towns. Unlike living in Charleston, which made finding a parking space a test of will.

Pratt's Insurance Agency was in a small two-story brick building on the main street, just a few doors down from Enid's shop. The agency was nestled between a small hardware store and a thrift shop, which Roo made a mental note to visit before leaving town.

When Roo walked in, Andy Pratt was on the phone,

laughing and running his hand through his thick, light brown hair. There wasn't anyone sitting at the front desk, so he held up a finger to Roo indicating he'd be with her soon. While Roo was waiting, she looked around the small office. Nearly every square inch of wall space was covered in small black frames containing photos of Pratt and various people. Some were taken at baseball games, one or two at what looked like a BBQ, and a few at weddings and various other locations. In each photo, Pratt was smiling, the quintessential small-town businessman, always on the prowl for new clients.

Pratt raised his finger again and gave Roo another smile, so she kept exploring. One photo caught her eye. She recognized the man from a photo in her file: Miller Blakeley. He and Pratt were holding up a string of fish, both beaming with pride at their catch. Roo reminded herself that the two of them knowing each other socially was to be expected in such a small town.

She turned around when she heard Pratt getting up from his desk. "Miss Murray, I presume. What a pleasure. I'm Andy Pratt. Sorry to keep you waiting. How can I help you?" He held out his hand.

Roo shook his hand, which was warm and damp. She hoped she had remembered to put hand sanitizer in her truck. "Nice to meet you too." She wiped her palm discretely on her pants leg. "As I mentioned when we talked yesterday, I'm investing Guinette Blakeley's death for the insurance company." She handed him her business card.

Pratt put his reading glasses on the end of his nose and read the card. "Well, I assume this is all just routine. Seems

like a pretty open-and-shut case to me. The coroner confirmed suicide, and the policy had passed the two-year
suicide exclusion clause." He removed his glasses. "So what
do you need from me?" His tone was less jovial now.

"May I sit?" Before Pratt replied, Roo had settled into
one of the wooden banker chairs in front of Pratt's desk.

"Of course." Pratt sat in his desk chair, the vinyl cushion
making a whooshing sound as he sat down.

"From the photo on your wall out there, it looks like you
are friends with Miller Blakeley, as well as being his insurance agent."

Pratt's eyes narrowed as he made a sweeping gesture with
his arms. "Look around town, Miss Murray. I'm the only
insurance agency here, and *everyone* knows everybody in this
place. That's what makes our little town so wonderful." He
leaned in slightly and lowered his voice to a near whisper.
"Don't tell anyone else. We'd like to keep our place special,
if you know what I mean."

"Oh, don't worry. I won't. Did you also know Guinette
personally also?"

Pratt's forehead creased slightly. "Well, yes. I mean, I
knew her. As I said, we're a small town."

"When Miller took out the policy on her, she didn't have
to undergo a physical. That's a bit unusual. I mean, a five-
million-dollar policy is fairly high for a woman who did only
volunteer charity work as far as I could tell, and they had no
children. Plus she seemed to be independently wealthy from
what I could find out. So why did Mr. Blakeley think he
would need five million dollars to bury her?"

Pratt's face grew redder. "Now look here, Miss Murray.

I appreciate that you have a job to do, but I don't appreciate the implications you're making."

"What implication is that? I think it's a fair question."

Pratt cleared his throat. "Well, you see . . ."

Roo flipped her file open. "The company says an underwriting exception was made for Mrs. Blakeley. At your request. Why did you ask them to waive the physical?" She stared at Pratt. "After all, Guinette was nearly sixty years old." Roo looked down at her file again. "It says here that the coroner who ruled her death a suicide was Ray Arnold." She looked up. "Do you know him well also?"

Pratt pushed his chair back slightly. "Well, yes. As a matter of fact, we're golfing buddies." He glanced at the clock on the wall. "I have a client coming in shortly. Are there any other questions you have? Because if not, I hope you can wrap this whole thing up soon. Miller has been through a lot, what with losing his wife and now having to endure this investigation."

"And waiting on his money?"

Pratt stood up. "I don't appreciate your tone, Miss Murray. But I wish you well, and I look forward to your final report soon."

CHAPTER 4

After leaving the insurance agency, Roo put her files under the seat of her truck and slathered on a generous helping of hand sanitizer.

When she walked into the thrift shop, a small bell hanging from the top of the door announced her entrance. A petite silver-haired woman appeared from the back of the shop. "Hello, dear. Please feel free to browse around. Miss Parker just brought in some more things from her mother's estate. Some lovely silver pieces you might like." She laughed. "Sorry, you're obviously not from around here, at least I've never seen you. So you probably don't know who Miss Parker is, or even care, for that matter."

"Thanks, I'll just look around." Roo pretended to look at the ornate silver candlesticks and a huge punch bowl. Whoever serves punch these days? "Lovely pieces, but I was hoping you might have some vintage hats. I'm going to a Mad Hatter party next month."

"Oh, how interesting. And where are you from?"

"Charleston. But I travel around the state a lot, so I'm rarely there."

"Well, I've only been there once. Lovely place, but so crowded."

"Yeah, parking's a bitch." When the lady frowned slightly, Roo made a mental note to watch her language. She was used to working in conservative small towns, but Blakeley was in a category all by itself from what she'd seen.

The woman motioned for Roo to follow her to a table in the rear of the store. "Here's a hat you might like. Miss Emily, our church pianist, wore it nearly every Sunday before she passed. Bless her heart."

Roo tried on the broad-brimmed pink hat. The white plastic flowers on the grosgrain ribbon hatband had long since lost their luster.

"There's a mirror over by the ladies' clothing section. Go take a look. It's lovely on you."

Roo stared at her image in the full-length mirror and managed not to laugh. Jeans, cowboy boots, a loose cotton top, and a funky vintage pink hat with awful plastic flowers. What a sight. "It's perfect. I'll take it."

"Would you like to look around some more?"

"Sure." Roo looked at a big antique magnifying glass, reminiscent of Sherlock Holmes. "I'll take this too. It'll make a good hostess gift for my friend."

The woman immediately picked up on the comment. "Oh?" You're staying here in Blakeley with friends?"

Roo had an appreciation for the soft interrogation techniques most small-town residents had honed. Suspicious of anyone showing up in town, they had learned how to covertly and charmingly ask, *what the hell are you doing in my town?*

After a brief moment of indecision, Roo decided to tell the truth. "Yes, Police Chief Hart and his wife are friends of mine." She detected a slight look of disapproval from the woman who was no doubt hoping Roo was staying with one of the town's more established and prominent residents.

"Ah, yes, what a lovely couple. They're new to our town, as you know. Considering our town's history, it's strange, don't you think, that a *newcomer* owns our only bookstore? Of course, that wasn't always true." The woman sighed.

"I'll take those two items now." Roo pointed to the hat and magnifying glass on the counter. "I assume you take credit cards?"

The woman threw her head back and laughed. "We're not that backward around here."

"Thanks. Oh, by the way, I recall reading in the *State* newspaper recently that one of your prominent citizens passed away."

The woman's smile was gone and her lips became a tight, thin line, with traces of the pink lipstick that matched the smear on a nearby coffee mug. "Why, yes. That is, I assume you're talking about Mrs. Blakeley, Miller's wife. Such an unfortunate situation."

"Since everyone seems to know each other here, I assume you knew her too. I'm sorry for your loss."

The woman looked away briefly and blinked back tears. "Yes, Guinette was a dear friend." She slid Roo's card through the card reader and handed it back to her. "No need to sign. Who'd recognize those screen scrawls anyway? Should I print you a receipt?"

"No, that's fine. May I ask—"

Before Roo could finish, the woman interrupted her. "I'm so sorry to be rude, but I need to get some things ready for the sidewalk sale." She put the two items in a large paper bag and handed it to Roo. "Please do come back. We get new items in almost every day." She walked away, leaving Roo standing at the register.

CHAPTER 5

Enid was standing on a small ladder dusting the top book-shelves when a young boy walked in. "Hello, can I help you find anything in particular?"

"Can I just look? I don't have any money."

Enid knew the nearest county library was at least twenty miles away. "Of course you can." She stepped off the ladder and pointed toward a small bookcase. "We don't carry too many young adult books since there aren't many of you in town, but here's what we have. You're welcome to stay awhile and read."

"Do you have a cat?"

Enid laughed. "No, what makes you ask?"

"I thought all bookstores have a cat. They kill the mice so they can't eat the books."

"Do you have a cat?" Enid asked.

He shook his head. "But Nana had two cats, Benjamin and Betsy."

"Oh, those are nice names."

"Yes, ma'am. But they gave them away when Nana died."

"I'm so sorry."

"Benjamin used to rub up my leg all the time. Nana said he was checking to see if I was a space alien." He giggled.

"The next time a cat does that, I'll know. Thanks for telling me." Enid pulled a book off the shelf. "Here's a book on UFOs, would you like to read that one?"

He grabbed the book from Enid's hand. "Wow. That's awesome." He flopped down into one of the reading chairs.

"You're welcome to stay here and read or you can also take it with you. You live next door, right?"

He nodded.

"I know you don't have money, so it's a loaner. You can bring it back when you finish."

Without looking up, the boy replied. "Thank you."

"I'll just get back to my dusting. Let me know if you need anything."

Suddenly, Roo burst through the front door, sending the warning bell into a frenzy. "Wow, this place is creepy."

"My bookstore?"

"No, silly. The whole town."

Enid nodded toward the boy who had mostly been swallowed by the large chair.

"Oh, sorry. I mean you have a great town, but it's . . ." Her voice trailed off.

A faint voice replied. "It's evil."

Roo looked at the young boy. "Evil? Well, that's a few shades worse than creepy. What makes you say that?"

Uncomfortable with where this conversation was headed, Enid tried to make eye contact with Roo. "I'm not sure this is an appropriate conversation for one of our guests." But Roo was already kneeling beside the boy's chair.

Ignoring Enid, Roo continued. "Why evil?"

"It killed Nana."

Roo glanced back at Enid, whose face was frowning. "The town killed your grandmother?"

Enid moved closer to the boy. "I'm sure he'd rather read,

so let's not bother him." Enid motioned with her head for Roo to move away from him.

He shrugged. "It's okay. Nobody believes me anyway."

Enid reached down and pulled on Roo's arm. "We need to talk." Then to the boy. "Sorry to bother you. We'll leave you alone and let you read now."

Roo pulled her arm away but followed Enid. When they were in the back room, Enid was the first to speak. "What were you thinking? He's just a boy."

"I wasn't attacking him or anything. Just having a friendly conversation."

"You know I adore you, but sometimes you can be too impulsive."

"Yeah, but what if he knows something about this town that we don't." She held out both arms, palms up. "What if some evil force has taken over this town and is killing people."

Enid laughed. "Oh, my. What an imagination you have. Maybe I should write—" Before she could finish, the boy pushed back the curtain that served as a door to the back area. "I have to go now. Can I really take this book?"

"Of course." Enid pulled a canvas book bag from one of the boxes. It had the store's logo on it. "You can take it in this. And just keep the tote as a gift."

"Thank you, ma'am." He turned to Roo. "Nana told me this town was evil. That's how I know." He dropped his head. "And now she's gone."

Before either Enid or Roo could respond, the boy fled from the store. Roo ran after him, just in time to catch a glimpse before he disappeared. "Damn. He went into the thrift shop I just left."

"He's been staying there with the owner. I guess since his grandmother died. I've seen him a few times, but I haven't seen him out often."

"Evil, huh?" Roo said. "Interesting."

CHAPTER 6

Josh transferred the perfectly seared fillets from the cast iron skillet to the three plates on the small kitchen island. "You ladies ready for the best salmon ever?"

Roo looked at Enid. "I thought you learned to cook. So why is your man doing all the work?"

Josh responded quickly. "I actually love to cook, and I don't get to cook for company often." He smiled at Enid. "Not that cooking for you isn't special too."

Roo shook her head. "I think he's a frigging AI thingie, a robot. No man is that good."

Enid laughed and said to Josh. "Are you happy now? She thinks you're too good to be true."

Enid finished mixing a salad dressing of coconut-infused balsamic vinegar and olive oil. She handed a small teaspoon to Roo. "Here, taste this and see if you like it. If not, I have some bottled dressing in the fridge."

Roo tasted it. "OMG! This is delicious. Okay, I guess you did learn to cook."

"I'd hardly say making a vinaigrette qualifies me as a cook, but thanks. There's a great store in Chapin that sells all kinds of olive oils and vinegars. It's a bit of a drive from down here, but I try to get up there every few months and stock up. The owner loves to give you samples of the various flavors."

"If I ever investigate a case in that part of the state, I'll be sure to stop in.'"

Josh put the plates on the table and Enid tossed the salad in a large bowl, while Roo took three wine glasses from the glass-front cabinet.

When all three were seated at the table, Josh offered a Native American blessing. Both of his parents were of Navaho descent, and Josh had been raised in their culture. "We give thanks to Great Spirit and to Mother Earth for producing this food, and to all those who labored to bring it to this table. Amen"

Roo threw her hands in the air and looked at Josh. "That was so much more meaningful than 'God is great. God is good . . .' Well, you know the rest."

Enid exchanged glances with Josh. "Any blessing is good, but I agree with you the Native American version is unique. And we're so glad you're here with us."

"We don't get a lot of visitors. You're welcome to stay as long as you'd like. In fact, I've got to take a short trip so you can keep Enid company while I'm gone."

Enid looked at Josh. "Is this—"

"Yeah, you know, police chief stuff. It'll only be a couple of days."

"Are you sure? I don't want to wear out my welcome, as Aunt Cat used to say."

Josh held up his wine glass. "I think we should toast Aunt Cat, Catherine Murray, for being the best aunt and a great town historian. Madden was lucky to have her."

Roo held up her glass. "Here's to Aunt Cat."

After the meal, Enid insisted on cleaning the kitchen but asked Josh if he'd prefer to clean his beloved skillet himself, which he promptly affirmed. "I hope Josh never has to decide between me and that skillet," she said to Roo.

"It belonged to my father and his father before that."

"The only time I cooked on a cast iron skillet, I was scraping food off for days," Roo said. "Just give me Teflon."

. . .

As Enid curled up next to Josh later that night, she whispered, "Are you asleep?"

Josh laughed softly. "Not anymore." He pulled her closer. "But you can wake me up anytime."

Enid kissed him before telling him about Roo's encounter with the young boy in the shop, and the boy's comment about the town being evil. "Do you know why he's staying next door? she asked.

"Sounds like Timmy . . . I can't remember his last name. He's the grandson of the Blakeleys' personal chef and assistant who died not long after Guinette passed."

Enid sat up in bed. "Wait, you mean Timmy's grandmother worked for the Blakeleys?" Before he could respond, she added, "And how do you know it's him?"

"If that's him, then yes, his grandmother worked for Guinette. I interviewed her after Guinette's death, and she mentioned her concern for her grandson Timmy."

"But what did she mean? Why was she concerned?"

"Sadly, she fell down the stairs and died a short time later." Josh kissed her hair. "But enough with all the questions. I took her comment to be natural grandmotherly concern, but I don't know what she was referring to. All I know is I need some sleep."

CHAPTER 7

Josh was gone the next morning before Enid got out of bed. As usual, he had left a note telling her not to worry. But she did. Even though she had agreed to move to Blakeley to support Josh, she knew the real reason they were here, and she was concerned.

On the surface, Blakeley was a sleepy little place time had passed by. Idyllic in many ways, like many small towns, it had its share of secrets, multi-generational grudges, and quaint traditions.

Buying the bookstore was Josh's way of giving her something to do until she figured out her own career. And it was also a way of integrating themselves into the close-knit town. But owning a business, no matter how small, was a mountain of paperwork, 24/7 attention to customer needs, complaints, leaky pipes, and endless phone calls. But neither of them expected to stay in Blakeley very long—a few years at most.

Having Roo visit was great. She was like the sister Enid never had, and like many sisters, the two were different in many ways. But Enid was also uneasy. Jack Johnson, who owned the *Tri-County Gazette* where Enid used to work as senior reporter, told her she had a sixth sense about knowing when something was going to turn into a big story. She was no longer a reporter, but that instinct was coming through loud and clear. Though Blakeley might not be evil, as Timmy's grandmother had suggested, something was amiss here.

Most days, she felt blessed for the convenience of living above the shop. Other days, like today, she wished she could drive to an office and immerse herself in mundane tasks. As much as she had complained to Jack about writing obituaries, her least favorite assignment at the paper, she also missed finding out more about the deceased and making their stories memorable. Halfway down the stairs, the smell of fresh coffee caught her attention. "Something smells good."

"I mixed a few of your coffee blends together. Hope you don't mind," Roo said.

"Mind? I love it. You'll have to give me your formula. I admit that even though I've learned to cook somewhat, I'm not a natural like you and Josh."

"And that lady, the one that owned this place, she dropped off these pastries a few minutes ago. OMG, they're so good. I had her leave a few extras, but I'll pay you."

"Don't be silly. I'm sure that made Tess happy."

They sat in the reading chairs, sipping coffee and munching on sweet buns. "Know what?" Roo asked.

Enid shook her head.

"You may not be a natural at cooking, although from what I can tell, you do pretty good, but you're great at sniffing out the truth."

Enid held up her hands in protest. "Don't go there. I'm not going to get involved in your investigation. For Josh's sake. I'm trying to start a new life, one that doesn't include investigation or getting myself in danger." Enid took another sip of coffee. "Besides, everyone, including the coroner, says Guinette's death was suicide. Even if you have doubts, you can't prove it."

"But what about the boy's grandmother?"

Enid frowned. "Now that's a stretch. How is she connected?"

"Because she worked for the woman whose death I'm investigating and then she died too."

"People die all the time. Let's not get carried away."

Roo crossed her arms on her chest. "You're in denial, that's what I think. You're trying to live this way-too-perfect life in a little town that's not perfect at all."

Enid frowned and began collecting empty cups. "Want more coffee?"

"His name is Timmy Sullivan, and his grandmother was Abigail Sullivan."

Enid sat down again. "That's what Josh said. But how do you know this?"

"You are getting rusty, girl. How many deaths do you think there are in this sleepy little town each year?" She held her palm up to Enid. "Wait, before you guess *hundreds,* it's only a few each year, so it was pretty easy to find her name. Timmy was listed as her only grandson in the obituary. Apparently, she was his guardian."

"You got all that from the obit?"

"You of all people should know that small-town newspapers love to print a person's life story when they die. In the bigger cities, it costs too friggin' much to print more than basic info. Anyway, her death was rumored to be suspicious also."

"How would you know that?"

"I found another article where she filed a police complaint a month before her death alleging she was being stalked. Someone broke into her house and stole a few things, but not enough to make it a serious robbery. More like an attempt to make it look like one. She told the police the town was evil. That made a good headline."

"But Josh would have been police chief then, and I'm sure he didn't investigate her break-in."

"According to the article, she lived on a rural route with a Blakeley address, so I guess the county sheriff would have investigated."

"Sheriff Wilson."

"You know him?"

Enid silently recalled all the times she and Josh had talked about the infamous sheriff. "Not personally, but Josh does."

"And? Is he on the up and up?"

Enid stood again. "As far as I know. I think I need another cup of coffee."

CHAPTER 8

After Roo left to talk to a man who had known Guinette well, Enid tidied up the kitchen and called Tess. "Can you watch the store for about half an hour? I need to run a few errands."

Tess lived a few blocks away and was always available to watch the store. Enid could tell how much she missed it.

When Tess arrived, Enid offered her a cup of coffee and explained she was only going next door to the thrift shop. And she didn't mention Timmy.

But since Enid had only been in the store a few times, she was long overdue paying her neighbor another visit.

Inside the shop, Enid was once again impressed with its tidiness. It wasn't easy to have so much stuff and yet be so well organized.

"Well, hello, neighbor. What brings you next door?"

"Just thought I'd stop by and look around," Enid said. "My houseguest said you had so many neat things in here. And, besides, it's been a while."

"Well, I'm glad you came in. Is there anything in particular you're looking for?"

Enid couldn't tell her what she really wanted, so instead she replied, "If it's okay with you, Petula, I'll just browse. But if you have anything special you'd like to show me, that would be great too."

"Actually, everyone calls me Pet for short." She smiled.

"I've always hated my given name, even as a child." She walked over to a display of crystal glasses. "These just came in today." She picked one up. "Very good quality, quite heavy."

"They're beautiful, but as you know we live in the small apartment over the bookstore, and I don't have much storage space."

Looking disappointed, Pet replied, "I see. Well, let's look at smaller items."

Enid spotted a basket filled with old fountain pens and vintage bookmarks. "These are interesting. I could use them in the store." Enid paused. "You know, yesterday a young boy about ten years old came in and borrowed a UFO book. Was that Timmy?"

"Yes, but are you saying he stole it?"

"Oh, no, certainly not. I told him to take it and return it when he was finished. I wondered if you could give him a message?"

A small crease formed between the woman's eyes. "Well, I suppose. What did you want to tell him?"

"I have a few more books I think he might be interested in. I wanted to invite him back to the store."

Pet's shoulders slumped. "He loves studying and reading. And Timmy never meets a stranger. I've told him to be careful about who he talks to. One day, it could be the wrong person." She appeared to force a smile. "But young kids these days don't understand how dangerous the world can be."

"Is Timmy a relative of yours?"

"Sadly, Timmy has no relatives left. He's in my care, but

I must say, most days, it's a bit overwhelming. I'm not a young woman, obviously."

"That's admirable, you know, that you're caring for Timmy. But I'm so sorry to hear he has no family. Are his parents deceased?"

"His mother and father were killed in a car accident when he was a baby, so his grandmother raised him until she died." Pet silently stared off into space. "I'm sorry, I got lost there for a moment. When she asked me to take care of him if something happened to her, I assumed she was just taking the usual precautions. I didn't realize it would happen so quickly."

"Sounds like you were very close. I'm sorry for your loss. That's quite a responsibility taking on raising a young child."

The bell hanging from the door rang as a man walked in. "Why don't you look around while I take care of this customer."

Enid picked out the best of the bookmarks and was examining an antique Mont Blanc pen when Pet returned. "He was looking for a silver teapot for his mother. We get very few of them these days. All the good stuff seems to have disappeared." She paused. "Where were we? Oh, yes. The strangest thing is that his grandmother fell down the stairs. It was as if she had a premonition something might happen. That's not so unusual, I guess. I have bad feelings sometimes, but luckily nothing usually comes of it."

Enid pretended to look more closely at the pen so she could consider her next move. Pet had been more forthcoming than Enid had expected, but if pushed too hard, Pet might shut down. "Poor Timmy must have been devastated when she died." She paused briefly. "His grandmother was Abigail Sullivan, is that right?"

Pet took a step back. "I'm sorry. You came in here to shop, and I've been pouring my heart out to you. I'll hush and let you look around."

Enid pulled some cash from her pocket. "I'd like to pay for these bookmarks."

Pet waived her hand. "Just take them. Consider them a very late welcome gift."

Enid tried to thank her, but Pet was already headed out the front door to check the items on the sidewalk table.

CHAPTER 9

Enid plopped a large brown paper shopping bag of groceries on the kitchen counter. With Josh still out of town, dinner would be for only her and Roo tonight. How much should she tell Roo about her visit with Pet? Although, there wasn't much to tell. But her reporting background had trained her to listen for what *wasn't said* as much as what was.

By the time Enid and Roo were sitting down to eat, Enid had convinced herself that there was no harm in sharing the visit to Pet with Roo.

"This is really good chicken, which is quite a feat. I eat so much chicken, and I'm usually sick of it. But this is tasty."

Enid laughed. "Stop it. You don't have to flatter me."

"Really, I'm not. What kind of seasoning is this?"

"Actually, I have no idea. Josh makes his own blend. I think it's cayenne pepper, paprika, and a few other things." Enid nibbled on a roasted asparagus spear. "How was your day?"

"My day was great, honey, how was yours?" The two women laughed. "Actually, it was pretty non-productive," Roo said. "I'm afraid I've hit the end of the road. I guess we'll have to pay Miller Blakeley, even though I *know* he killed his wife."

"That's a strong accusation." Enid paused, still debating whether she wanted to share her own doubts. "But I can understand why you might be suspicious."

Roo put her fork down and slapped her palms on the table. "I knew it. You've found out something, haven't you? Enid is alive and well in Stepford."

"Stop it. Blakeley is *not* like Stepford. It's just different, that's all. And besides, I just thought it was time to visit my shop neighbor."

Roo leaned in closer. "And what did you find out?"

"Well, Pet, that the owner's name—"

"That's a weird name."

"It's short for Petula, you know, like Petula Clark."

"Who?"

"Not important. Anyway, Pet and I had a good chat. It seems she agreed to become Timmy's guardian before Abigail Sullivan died."

"How's that?"

"Pet thinks Abigail had a premonition something would happen to her and asked her to take care of Timmy if necessary. Pet probably agreed because she didn't take Abigail's concerns seriously."

"Did Abigail tell her what she was afraid of?"

"Pet didn't say she was afraid, just that Abigail thought something could happen and since Timmy had no other relatives, she wanted to be sure he was taken care of."

"That's more than she would have told me. What else?"

"I think I pushed her too hard and she shut down. When I asked her if Abigail Sullivan was Timmy's grandmother, it was like a steel wall fell between us. The conversation ended abruptly."

"That's exactly what happened with me yesterday. So why is she so uncomfortable talking with us? I always thought shop owners loved to share small-town gossip, you know, being lonely and all that."

Enid laughed. "You watch too much TV. But she is uncomfortable, for whatever reason."

Roo crammed a hunk of chicken in her mouth and held up a finger to ask for a minute to finish chewing before she resumed. "I need to know more about Abigail. It might help me find out something about Guinette Blakeley's so-called suicide."

Enid sipped her tea. "Please remember, you are a guest in this house and in this town. These people don't like any kind of strangers, especially nosy ones. And we've got to be respectful of Josh's situation."

"I can find a hotel. Seriously. No hard feelings."

Enid put her hand on Roo's. "Don't be silly. I'm just asking you not to push too hard. I'd hate for someone to call Josh and complain about you."

Roo offered a mock salute. "Yes, ma'am. Now can I have another piece of that scrumptious chicken?"

CHAPTER 10

The next day after breakfast with Roo, Enid opened the shop and sat down with a cup of another one of Roo's blends. This one clearly had cinnamon in it and was just as good as yesterday's concoction. Enid made a mental note to include both blends on the shop's small menu of coffees and teas.

Roo had made it clear she was going to keep digging until her time ran out. Once she gave the okay for the company to pay Miller Blakeley, there was no legitimate reason for Roo to continue looking into Abigail Sullivan's death. Enid hoped nothing further would come of Roo's suspicions.

But something was clearly off about the whole affair. Enid decided to call an old friend. Blakeley wasn't one of the areas covered by the *Tri-County Gazette,* but its editor and her former boss, Jack Johnson, might know something. It was hard for her to admit she had purposefully avoided contact with her dearest friend and wasn't sure why she had.

After four rings, Enid was about to end the call.

"Hello. Enid? Is that really you?" said the familiar voice.

"Hi, Jack. Yep, it's me. How are you?"

"Well, I'm just peachy. The real question is how are you? And where the hell are you anyway? Someone told me Josh was a police chief in some weird little place not far from the coast."

Enid laughed. "I've missed you, and I'm sorry I haven't

been in touch. Josh and I are living in Blakeley, and yes, he's the police chief, although this place is so small it's really a part-time position."

"Please tell me he's not gardening in his spare time."

For the next ten minutes, Enid told Jack about their life in Blakeley. "And guess who's staying with us right now? Roo," she added without waiting for a reply.

"Roo? The insurance investigator?"

"She's here looking into Guinette Blakeley's suicide."

"Seemed open and shut from what I heard."

"Well, Roo isn't so sure. But the reason I called is about another case that didn't get much coverage. I wanted to know if you had heard anything about Abigail Sullivan."

"Abigail Sullivan," Jack repeated. "I can't recall the name. Who was she?"

"She was Guinette's personal chef and administrative assistant. Died last year. Apparently, she fell down a flight of stairs."

"That's too bad. Obviously, you must think there's some connection or you wouldn't be asking. And, by the way, why are you asking? Are you reporting again?"

Enid laughed. "Oh, no. I'm just helping Roo. But there's something off about this whole affair. And I want to satisfy my own curiosity."

"Want your old job back?"

"No, but thanks. And by the way, how's Ginger doing?"

"I think she's going to be a great reporter. She's still got a lot to learn, but you gave her such a head start before you left. Thanks for all you did to give her confidence and help her learn the ropes. As you know, she's a great researcher, which is a big part of the job. Want me to see what she can dig up?"

"That would be great. And I hate to impose, but can she do it quickly? Roo's got a short time left to close out her investigation, and if the two cases are connected, it might buy her some time."

"I'll get Ginger right on it. You know she'd do anything for you."

"By the way, I assume you never found another buyer for the paper after the deal with your old Chicago friend fell through."

"Nah, haven't really looked for one. What would I do with all that extra time and money? Besides, the fish aren't biting too good around here these days." He paused. "I miss you. Let's plan to get together when Josh returns. It's not that long of a drive to Blakeley."

"Sounds good. I miss you too."

As soon as Enid put her phone down, the faint jingle of the bells on the door signaled someone trying to get in. The store hadn't opened yet, but when she saw it was Pet, Enid let her in.

"I'm so sorry to bother you this early. If you're like me, you need this quiet time to get everything in order, because once the doors open, there's no time to do anything."

Enid laughed. "I wish we were that busy." She motioned toward one of the reading chairs. "Come in and have a seat. I'll get you a cup of coffee."

Instead of sitting immediately, Pet examined the titles on the bookshelves. "I should come in here more often. You have some great books." She sighed. "Sadly, I have little time to read now that . . ."

Enid put a cup of coffee on the table. "I'm sure taking care of Timmy must be difficult, especially since there are no other relatives to help you."

Pet took a sip of coffee. "This is marvelous. I definitely want to get some of this blend. What's it called."

"It's Roo's blend, but I'm going to ask her to share it with me. I'll bring you some when it's ready."

"That hint of cinnamon does the trick." Pet took another sip. "Your guest is a bit impertinent, but I guess that's alright these days. Young people baffle me. As I said, Timmy has no one else as far as I can tell, and I could never live with myself if I put him in foster care. After all, I promised Abigail."

Pet glanced around the room, appearing to be lost in her thoughts. "But I guess you're wondering why I'm here. Although I must say, we must make a pact to do this more often. Visit each other, I mean." She cleared her throat. "I don't know how else to say this. I looked you up after you came to see me and saw that you had been a reporter and solved a few cases. That's impressive."

"Thank you, but I had a lot of help."

"Nonetheless, I would like to hire you."

Enid sat up in her chair. "Hire me? For what? Do you want an article about the shop?"

Pet shook her head. "Oh, no, my dear. I want you to investigate Abigail's death. Actually, I think she was murdered." She exhaled loudly. "There, I've said it."

"I'm not sure how to respond. But first, let me say, I'm not a licensed investigator. You need to hire someone experienced in these matters. Besides, Josh is the chief of police, so I hardly think it would be appropriate for me to get involved."

"So, Chief Hart is investigating Abigail's death then?"

"No, but I mean, I don't know. But even if he were, I couldn't talk about it. But I am curious as to why you think she was murdered."

Pet pulled a tissue from the pocket of her trousers and was fingering it. "But you see, that's the problem. I don't *know* anything. It's just a feeling. And if I hire an investigator, he or she will need something to go on, a place to start."

"As would I. You can't investigate a feeling without someplace to start looking." Enid's mind flooded with memories of the times she had begun an investigation with only a hunch. "But you should talk with someone about it, just to put your mind at ease. It's only natural to have thoughts bouncing around in your head. Usually they don't pan out." Considering how Enid felt something was off, she felt guilty minimizing Pet's suspicions.

Pet glanced at her watch. "Well, I guess I'd better go open the shop. Thanks for listening. And please don't tell your husband what I said. It probably is just an old woman's crazy thoughts." She stood to leave. "And I'd love to get some of that coffee when you blend it."

Enid followed Pet to the door. "Would you be willing to talk to Roo? She's a licensed investigator, and I've worked with her. She'll keep everything to herself."

"Well, . . ." Pet hesitated. "Are you sure? I have to live here and I can't risk ruining my reputation in this town. But on the other hand, I do owe it to Abigail to put my fears to rest."

"Roo will be back later this afternoon. Why don't you come over when you close the shop? Bring Timmy with you. He can watch TV upstairs while we talk."

After Enid closed the door behind Pet, she felt a familiar sense of dread overcome her.

CHAPTER 11

Business had been good that day at the bookshop, and Enid was looking at the store's transactions on SquareUp when Roo came in and flopped into one of the chairs. "I'm exhausted. What a day."

"So did you learn anything?"

"Hell, yeah. I learned I never want to live in a small town. Too weird."

"Well, Blakeley is even more unusual than most small towns. But there are good people here too."

Roo pulled an apple from her briefcase and took a big bite. "I'm starving. If there was a decent restaurant in this place, I'd take you out."

"Roland's is a good cafe, but it closes at 2:00 pm. I've got some shrimp and a box of pasta. We can make a decent meal with that."

"Sounds delish."

"Besides Pet is coming to talk to you when she closes the shop."

"Pet, you mean that weirdo next door?"

"Roo, don't be so judgmental. Pet's having a hard time taking care of Timmy and running the shop. Besides, she wants to talk to you about Guinette Blakeley's personal assistant."

Roo jumped up from her seat. "Really? Do you think she knows something?"

"Why don't we go upstairs and you can relax while I start dinner. And then I'll tell you all about my conversation with Pet."

"I'd like to cook, if you're good with that. You won't let me pay you for staying here, so it's the least I can do." She reached down and pulled a bottle of wine from a paper bag. "And I've got the booze, so be nice to me. Had to go to the next town to buy it though. Like I said, Blakeley is weird."

• • •

After dinner, Enid was putting the last of the dishes away when the door buzzer rang. "That's probably Pet. I'll get it."

Enid looked through the glass door and opened it. "Come on in, we were just cleaning up the dinner dishes."

"I can come back later—"

"No, come on up. Roo is anxious to talk to you. We can take the freight elevator if you'd rather not climb these steep stairs."

Pet smiled. "I'm used to it. My building is older than yours. Go on, I'll follow you."

When they reached the top of the stairs, Roo was wiping the walnut counter with a dishtowel.

"Roo, you remember Petula?"

"I'd prefer Pet," she said smiling. "Pet and Roo, what a combo of names."

"I guess you didn't like Petula any more than I liked Ruby-Grace." The two women laughed together, relieving Enid's tension, considering their first encounter didn't go as smoothly.

Enid got everyone settled and brought three cups of coffee. "I've only recently started drinking coffee, but I do enjoy a good cup after dinner."

Roo sat up straight in her chair. "Okay, enough of this getting-to-know-each-other stuff, let's talk real. Why do you think Abigail Sullivan was murdered?"

Pet smiled and nodded. "I'm beginning to like you because you're a woman who talks straight." She sipped her coffee. "Anyway, just before Abigail died, she made me promise I'd take care of Timmy, her grandson, if anything happened. She was the only mother he had ever known."

"That's not unusual for someone to make arrangements for the care of their child. Why is that suspicious to you?" Enid asked.

"You're right, but the timing of it, and the rest of our conversation now makes me wonder."

Roo waved her hand in a circle urging Pet to continue. "Go on."

"As I told you, Abigail was the private chef and personal assistant to Guinette Blakeley."

"That's a weird combo, chef and personal assistant," Roo said.

Pet nodded. "This is not New York, as you know, so we don't have many chefs for hire. Anyway, Abigail wanted to put away as much savings as she could for Timmy's college fund. Besides, she told me Guinette ate mostly salads at lunch, and that no-good husband of hers was rarely home for dinner. So Abigail really only cooked a couple of simple meals a day."

"You're talking about Miller Blakeley, right?" Roo asked.

Pet nodded. "As part of Abigail's duties, she paid the household bills and balanced Guinette's personal bank accounts. All the bills were paid from those."

"You mean Guinette paid all the household bills?" Enid asked.

"Oh, no. I said they were paid from her accounts, but Miller was supposed to deposit money in her account to cover his share of them. And sometimes he did."

"The few times Guinette came here to the bookstore, she was dressed in expensive clothes," Enid said.

"Yes, Miller saw to it that his wife gave the right impression wherever she went." Her voice lowered. "Even if it was a front. Jointly, they were nearly broke. Or at least he was. But Guinette had her own funds, which she kept separate. That was part of Abigail's job—to oversee those funds."

Roo almost came out of her chair. "I knew Miller had financial problems, although almost everyone I talked to indicated the Blakeleys owned nearly everything in town."

"Miller wanted to own *everyone*. That was his power."

Roo and Enid glanced at each other. "What do you mean?" Enid asked.

Pet took a deep breath and glanced around the room. "You've done a great job decorating this upstairs suite. Perhaps I can get you to give me some pointers."

Roo leaned forward in her chair. "How did Miller own everyone? And why was he broke? Are you saying he had something on the town folks?" She looked at Enid. "I told you this place was weird."

"I'm saying he had a way of pulling people in and learning all about them. Then they were afraid to cross him." Pet paused. "And whatever he personally made on his investments was spent on drugs, especially in the last few years."

Roo jumped up and grabbed a folder from her briefcase. She flipped through several pages and pointed. "I know Miller was addicted to prescription drugs, Oxy specifically. His so-called doctor kept him supplied legally." She read a few more lines. "I wonder if Dr. Edwards, Miller's doctor, is related to the dentist down the street. I saw his sign on the building."

"Dr. Edwards is the dentist, and he prescribed most of the medications for Miller."

"A dentist? But how could he?" Roo asked. "Wait, I forgot. This is Blakeley. You can do anything in a town you own."

"Abigail said Miller had some dental surgery and Dr. Edwards gave him pain pills." Pet said. "Miller kept going back for more and Dr. Edwards was happy to oblige."

Roo looked at Enid. *"We've* got some work to do."

· · ·

After Pet left, Roo and Enid were finishing up the dishes when Enid's phone rang. The screen showed the photo of a familiar face. "Ginger, hello."

"Hey, girl. I can't believe I'm actually talking to you. Why haven't you been in touch?"

"I'm sorry, it's just that—"

"Never mind, I know you have a new life now. How's Josh? Wonderful and handsome as ever, I assume?"

Enid laughed. "He's great. I'll tell him you asked about

him. He's out of town right now, working."

"Well, as much as I want to catch up, I'm sure you want to know what I found out. I called a few people I know and promised them I wasn't doing a story, only asking for a friend." She exhaled loudly. "Whew, all I can say, for a small town, Blakeley is a hotbed of intrigue."

"I agree," Roo called out loud enough for Ginger to hear.

"Ginger, you remember Roo, Catherine Murray's niece? She's staying with me for a few days."

"Hey, Roo, of course I remember you. So, anyway, everyone I talked to raised suspicions about Abigail Sullivan's death. Some of them suggested she knew too much. One person, whose identity I swore I would protect, said he was sure she was pushed down the stairs."

"By whom?" Roo said, raising her voice again to be heard.

"My informant didn't go so far as to say who he thought did it, but he didn't have anything good to say about Miller Blakeley, that's for sure."

"Even though these are suspicions and not evidence, it implies a possible connection between Abigail's and Guinette's deaths," Enid said. "If you learn anything else, please let me know. And I promise to come to Madden for a visit before too long. I guess Jack told you I own a small bookstore and coffee shop, so it's hard for me to get away."

"I'm holding you to that promise," Ginger said. "And I only promised I wasn't doing an article. When you and Roo get to the bottom of all this, *you* can write an article for the *Tri-County Gazette* as a guest reporter."

"I'm not working on this case, Roo is."

Ginger and Roo both laughed. "Yeah, right, girlfriend." Ginger said. "Talk later."

Roo's phone pinged and she looked at the screen. "Damn. Got a text from my boss. He says to wrap it up and recommend payment to Miller Blakeley." She slammed the phone down on the table. "We've got to do something. I'm not recommending payment to a guy who killed two women."

"You don't know that for sure. But I think it's time to bring Josh into this conversation."

CHAPTER 12

After taking a shower and putting on her nightgown, Enid looked at the time. Josh would be calling soon for his nightly check-in. She missed him and looked forward to hearing his voice. What she didn't look forward to was telling him Pet's suspicions about the most prominent citizen in the town."

At the appointed time, the phone rang. "Hi, babe. Miss you. How's everything? You holding down the fort for me?"

"Yeah, but I miss you too." She paused. "When will you be home?"

"Why? Is something wrong?"

"No, but we need to talk."

"How about ten minutes?"

"What do you mean?"

"I decided to come home tonight. I just entered the town limits. I only called to make sure you don't shoot me when I come in the door."

Enid breathed a sigh of relief. "I promise not to shoot you."

After the call, Enid knocked on the guest room door. "Hey, Roo. Hope you're still awake. Just wanted to tell you Josh will be here in a few minutes. Didn't want you to be surprised."

Roo opened the door, wearing her long sleep shirt. "Oh, that's good. We can tell him—"

"No, it can wait until the morning, and I need to talk to

him first."

Roo made a face before she shut the door. "Oh, alright. Good night, then."

A few minutes later, Josh came in. Rushing up the stairs, he pulled Enid to him. "Where's Roo?"

"In the guest room."

"Good, then I can do what I want to," he said grinning."

Enid pushed him away gently. "But why are you back early? Is everything alright?"

"Depends. I got a call from the mayor that Miller Blakeley was concerned about some 'crazy woman' going around town asking embarrassing questions about Guinette's death." He nodded toward the guest room. "You don't suppose she's talking about Roo, do you? Or is there another crazy out-of-towner visiting Blakeley and staying with my wife?"

"Ouch. Want to talk now or should we wait until morning?" Enid asked.

"Now's good for me. I'm too excited about being home to go to sleep. I'll make some coffee."

When the coffee was ready, Enid suggested they take it to the balcony at the back of their upstairs apartment. The area was small—just enough space for two chairs, the director kind with folding wooden frames and fabric sling seats. They were a wedding present from Ginger and had "Enid & Josh" embroidered on the back panels.

"It's so nice out here. I love the cool night air," Josh said.

Enid pulled her sweater closer. "It'll soon be too cold to enjoy being out."

Josh set his coffee on the tiny table between them and

took Enid's hand. "Do you miss our old place and the big porch we used to sit on?"

Enid squeezed his hand. "Sometimes, if I'm honest with myself." She paused. "And I miss my friends. It's hard to get close to anyone here. We're such outsiders. But I love the bookstore and coffee shop. We have some good days, but I'm surprised we don't have more of them, more consistent sales. Especially considering the town's history."

"It's not the same place Miller's great-grandfather founded. And as you know, most people are too busy to read these days."

"Yes, I know. But I told you I'm happy anywhere you're happy. Are you?"

Josh picked up his coffee mug and took a few sips. "What makes me happy is doing meaningful work, feeling like I'm contributing to the good of society." He released Enid's hand and leaned over in his chair, running his hands through his hair. "These days, I'm not sure."

"I know we agreed not to talk specifics about why you're here, and I accepted that. But if you're not happy, you need to let me know."

Josh leaned back in his chair. "I hate keeping secrets from you, but that was a condition of my taking this assignment, and it's also safer for you not to know."

Enid slapped at a small no-see-um bug on her arm. Smaller than a flea, these tiny bugs suck blood like mosquitoes and are especially prevalent in the warmer areas of the South. "I had planned to talk to you tomorrow about Roo's investigation, but I think I need to tell you a few things."

"Uh oh. I'm starting to have deja vu. Have you gotten

yourself involved in her case?"

"No, well, I mean not exactly. I've told her several times that because you're the police chief, I have to stay out of it."

"But . . .?"

"But I think she's right about Miller Blakeley." She paused. "Roo thinks he killed both his wife and her personal assistant, or at least had them killed."

Josh sat up straight. "Whoa. That's pretty strong. Does she have any proof?"

Enid shook her head and told him about her conversation with Ginger. "And now she's getting pressure from the insurance company to sign off on the investigation and approve payment."

"Can you blame them? Unless she has something concrete that can be investigated, she'll have no choice. Besides, Roo can be a little, let's say, excitable at times."

Enid laughed. "That's part of her charm. But, yes, you're right. The woman who owns the shop next door, Petula, is now raising Abigail Sullivan's grandson. Pet, that's what she prefers to be called, thinks Miller is guilty too."

Josh grinned. "That'll teach me to go out of town and leave you with Roo. I should have known you two would get into trouble." He took a sip of cold coffee and made a face. "Ugh, that's nasty. I've never understood people who drink iced coffee." He glanced at his watch, an old-fashioned analog model that belonged to his father. "It's getting late, but I need to tell you a few things. Then we can sleep on what to do about it."

Enid nodded. "Okay."

"When I asked you to come here to live in Blakeley, I

promised it would only be a couple of years at most. When we left Madden and Governor Larkin heard I was available, he called me and asked me to rejoin the gang task force, but this time on my terms."

"You mean the same governor who told you to break up with me because of a conflict of interest."

Josh laughed. "Yep, same charming guy."

"Was I included in the 'on your own terms' part of the agreement?"

Josh held up two fingers to indicate about an inch. "Only about this much. He knows we're married and that you're no longer a reporter. The rest of the agreement had to do with not calling me in for all those meetings and trying to force me into being a political lap dog."

"Wow. That was a big concession for him. What did you have to give him in return? Or do I want to know?"

Josh threw his arms and made a sweeping gesture. "Look at this town. It's quiet, quaint, has an interesting history. It's idyllic. Or at least it should be."

"But . . .? Enid asked.

"Anytime one person becomes so influential in an area, there's the potential for corruption."

"Are you investigating Miller? Or should I not ask?"

"You shouldn't, but I'll tell you anyway. But you have to promise not to tell Roo anything I'm telling you."

"I promise."

"As part of my assignment on the gang task force, the governor asked me to investigate possible gang involvement, or at least drug trafficking, here."

"Here? That's odd. I haven't seen any signs of a drug

problem."

Josh tapped the tip of her nose with his finger. "You're very perceptive. I think the real target of his investigation is Miller himself."

"Do *you* think he's involved in drug trafficking?"

"I'm not sure. I think he's dirty, but I can't get enough concrete information to confirm my suspicions."

"But . . . I don't know why he sent you here. Why doesn't the South Carolina Law Enforcement Division investigate? Wouldn't that be their responsibility?"

"He could refer the case to them, yes. But I think he was afraid to make the investigation official until he knew if there was something to it. If he had told me the truth about this assignment, I might have refused it. Talk about a political hotbed! Miller has been a big campaign contributor to many of the who's who in this state, including the governor himself."

"So he wanted to be sure before he cut off his own funding."

"Damn, you're smart," Josh said, grinning.

"We need to sleep on this. Somehow, we've got to let Roo know that even if she's forced to approve payment on his wife's insurance policy, Miller is still under investigation."

CHAPTER 13

The next morning, Enid woke up to the aroma of bacon and coffee. Josh loved to cook and Enid missed his cooking when he was gone, even if he didn't always make the healthiest of choices.

Enid slipped into jeans and a long-sleeved T-shirt to join him.

Josh flipped a strip of bacon in his prized skillet. "Now that's what I like—my women barefoot and in the kitchen."

Enid picked up a dishrag on the counter and slapped him with it. "Stop it. You're the least chauvinistic man I know."

Josh kissed her on the cheek. "Thank you. I try."

"Oh for Pete's sake. Take it back to the bedroom," said Roo, who was sitting on the sofa.

"Oh, hey, Roo. I didn't see you," Enid said.

"Don't mind me. I'm just jealous of all this domestic bliss."

Josh turned to Enid. "Roo and I have been catching up while you were sleeping."

"Sorry, I'm not used to staying up that late, so I overslept. What did I miss?"

Josh and Enid exchanged glances. "She was telling me about not wanting to authorize payment to Miller."

Enid looked at Roo. "Karma is a powerful thing. Even if he gets paid, and *if* he's involved somehow in Guinette's and Abigail's deaths, he'll eventually pay for it."

Roo jumped up from the sofa. "Okay, now I know something's going on. The Enid I know would demand that we find out what happened and hold him accountable. So where is *that* Enid?"

Enid glanced at Josh again and then back to Roo. "I told you, I cannot get involved. I don't want to. I'm just a shop owner now."

"Riiiiight," Roo said.

Josh's cell phone rang and he glanced at the screen. "I need to get this. You ladies go ahead and eat without me." He answered his phone while putting the last piece of bacon on a paper towel to drain and then walked outside on the balcony and shut the door behind him.

Enid cut slices from a loaf of Tess's homemade bread and popped it in the toaster. Roo looked for butter in the refrigerator. "I found some real butter, but you don't eat the real stuff, as I recall. I remember that god-awful plant-based stuff you had one time."

Enid laughed. "Thanks to Josh's bad influence, I've been converted."

"My goodness, will wonders never cease." Roo put the crock of butter on the table and rummaged in the silverware drawer for a butter knife.

Enid put out the plates and then glanced at Josh outside. She could tell from his body language something was going on.

When he walked back inside, he said, "I've got to go." He picked up a piece of bacon and munched it.

"Is everything okay?" Enid asked.

As Josh walked down the stairs, he called over his

shoulder. "I'll fill you in later."

"I'll do the dishes, you go on downstairs and open up," Roo said."

Enid glanced at the time on her watch. "Oh, my goodness. It's later than I thought."

"I'll probably be out of your hair soon. Looks like I'm going to have to admit defeat and turn in my report."

Enid put her arm around Roo's shoulder. "Karma. Trust me."

Before running downstairs, Enid brushed her hair and quickly put on some mascara. As soon as she pulled up the shade on the shop door and glanced outside, she called Roo. "Come here. Quick."

Roo ran down the stairs. "What's going on?"

Enid pointed outside. "I'm not sure, but Josh is next door at Pet's shop. That's his SUV."

"Come on, let's see what's going on," Roo said.

Enid grabbed Roo's arm. "No, we need to wait until—"

But Roo pulled away and ran out the door. Pet was standing on the sidewalk. "What's going on?" Roo asked. "Why are you out here?" Roo tried to see inside the shop window.

Enid walked out to join them. It was pointless to admonish Roo, so she focused on Pet. "Are you alright? Here, take my sweater. You're shivering."

"I'm fine. No one was hurt."

Roo and Enid looked at each other. "What do you mean?" Roo asked.

"Someone broke into the upstairs apartment. Timmy and I sometimes stay at my family farm not too far from here. We have a man and his wife who take care of it in exchange for staying in the small cabin nearby. The farm still has a few goats and chickens. Timmy loves to feed them."

Roo put her hands on her hips. "But what happened?"

"Roo, we shouldn't get involved in this. Josh is here, so everything is under control."

Pet lowered her head and sobbed softly. "I'm just thankful we weren't here."

"Was anything taken?" Enid asked.

"Not that I can tell. The place was ransacked."

"Sounds like they were looking for something," Roo said.

Josh walked over to where they were standing, directing his attention to Pet. "The sheriff's office won't send a crime scene investigator out for a routine break-in, and the shop is likely full of hundreds of prints from customers. We don't have much to go on."

Enid took Roo's arm. Come on, we're interfering. I know that look on Josh's face." Enid hugged Pet. "If you need me, you know where I am."

• • •

Roo sat in one of the reading chairs in the shop with her arms folded across her chest. "It's not right."

Enid sat in the other chair across from her. "What's not?"

"I *know* Miller had someone break in, but I don't know what they were looking for." Enid looked around the shop. She knew it was never going to be a permanent home for her and Josh, but lately she was feeling like the earth was moving beneath her, causing her to feel unsteady and vulnerable. For years, as a reporter, she longed for a simple, normal life—the kind of life other people had. And she almost had it.

But now, her world was shifting again. She could feel it, and it wouldn't be long before she and Josh would have to move on. Enid felt sorrier for him than for herself. He loved law enforcement, but he hated politics, and sometimes the two were inseparable. "You're going to have to let the authorities work this out."

Before Roo could reply, Josh walked in. "Look, I know you're upset," he said to Roo. "You want to get the bad guys and so do I. But justice is sometimes slow."

"Do you think Miller Blakeley was involved in this?" Roo asked Josh.

"We have nothing at this point to tie him to it. What makes you think he's involved?" Josh asked.

Roo jumped from her chair. "So there's no case against him? I mean you're not going to let this drop, are you?"

Josh laughed. "No, I won't, and yes, there's a case. Now please, let me do my job." He looked at Enid. "Talk to her. I've got to get back to work."

After Josh left, Roo said to Enid, "I'll pack my bags and leave shortly. I'll complete my report authorizing payment and drop it off at the post office on the way home. Miller Blakeley will get paid for killing his wife, and probably Abigail Sullivan too."

CHAPTER 14

Enid played with the salad on her plate, pushing the lettuce around and lining up the small pieces of tomato.

"What's on your mind?" Josh asked. "You haven't said a thing since I've been home. Are you upset because I told you and Roo to stay out of this case?"

Enid pushed her plate away. "No, you were right. I shouldn't have invited Roo to stay here."

"I thought you liked her."

"I do. I like her a lot, but it's hard for me not to get involved."

"Because of me?" Josh paused. "Or because you miss being a reporter?"

Enid put her hand on Josh's. "I want you to be happy. If it means being the police chief in Blakeley, then we need to make that work."

"But do you enjoy having the bookstore?"

Enid smiled. "Let's have a glass of wine on the balcony. It suddenly feels stuffy in here."

When they had settled in their chairs outside, Josh poured them each a glass of chardonnay. "I like Roo. She's lively, I'll give her that." He tipped his glass to Enid's. "Here's to us and doing whatever it takes for *us* to be happy."

"I'll drink to that." Enid took a small sip. "Blakeley is a charming town, at least that's what the town's website says."

She laughed. "But there's also a sinister feeling here. I've felt it since we arrived. Maybe it's just because we're outsiders. I doubt we'll ever be accepted, not in the way the descendants of the founding families are."

"Do you miss belonging somewhere? I know I do at times."

Enid set her glass on the small table between them and turned in her seat to face him. "I want you to know I'm *not* unhappy. Not at all. Just restless, I suppose. When you're gone it gets lonely, especially on those days when the shop isn't busy. That's why I enjoyed Roo being here."

Josh sighed. "There's never a good time to say this, but I've got to leave again. I may be gone a couple of days, depending on whether I can get in to see Larkin and where our conversation goes. This may be the last time, though."

"Are you going undercover again?"

He smiled. "No, I'm too well known in the state now, thanks to a reporter whose name I won't mention. But I need to wrap up my investigation." He took a sip of wine. "What was it you told Roo? Karma? I'm going to make some Karma happen."

• • •

On the drive to Columbia, Josh had time to think. Too much time. Normally, he was a man of action, believing you can spend too much time in your head. But today, he needed to think through what he was going to say to Governor Larkin.

Along the way, Josh admired the countryside, which later

gave way to the busy streets of the capital city. After dodging a road repair truck and dozens of USC students walking with earbuds drowning out the rest of their world, he found a parking spot near the state house where the governor's office was located.

After signing in and going through a metal detector, Josh was escorted to the lower lobby and down the hall. "The governor will be with you shortly," an assistant said.

Josh was leafing through a brochure about state government in the waiting area when the assistant summoned him. "Governor Larkin will see you now."

Larkin was seated at the large mahogany desk. "Josh, how good to see you. Please have a seat. Would you like coffee or tea?"

Josh shook his head. "No thanks, I'm good."

Larkin leaned back in his chair. "I must say I was a bit taken aback when you requested an urgent meeting today. Are you and Mrs. Hart both okay?"

"Enid and I are fine, but thanks for asking. And thanks for seeing me on short notice. I know you're busy." Josh paused. "We've had an incident in Blakeley I think you need to be aware of." For the next few minutes, Josh filled the governor in on Roo's investigation and the break-in at Pet's shop.

"Well, that's unfortunate. I hope no one was injured."

"She and the boy were not home at the time."

"So why the urgency? And how is it connected to our work?" Larkin tapped his fingertips on the desk, one by one. Impatience or anxiety? Josh wasn't sure.

"I need to know the truth, sir."

"I see." Larkin tapped his fingers again and his eyes narrowed. "You're a smart man, Josh, so I'm sure you've put some of the pieces together. Please understand that my intention was never to withhold information, but only to share what I thought was relevant."

Josh took a few deep breaths. He knew from experience that confronting Larkin and pushing him into a corner just made things worse. "You've asked me to investigate possible drug dealings in Blakeley. Have you ever been there, sir?"

"I think I may have been there a few years back during a campaign."

Josh hesitated. "To see Miller Blakeley?"

Before Larkin could respond, the governor's assistant came in. "You have a meeting in five minutes, sir."

Larkin drummed his fingertips on the desk again. "Tell them we'll have to reschedule or they'll have to wait. I need to finish up here." After the assistant left, Larkin turned his attention back to Josh. "You're implying, I believe, that I'm beholden to Miller because he contributed to my campaign."

"Not beholden, sir. Just that you do have a relationship with him. Blakeley is a small, somewhat charming town. I'm sure you know its history, that it was founded by the Blakeley family as a writers' village. Now it's just a nice little town with a few descendants of the original founding families and a smattering of newcomers, like me. At this point, I've found no evidence of large-scale organized drug dealings. I understand Miller may have a drug dependency problem related to a past surgery."

"Go on."

"So why don't you tell me what you're really looking for

in Blakeley so we can speak openly."

Larkin smiled, the same smile he used during political speeches. "I thought that's what we were doing."

Josh cleared his throat. "Is Miller Blakeley the target of your investigation?"

"Should he be?" Larkin drummed his fingertips again. "Or perhaps I should ask if that's what you think or is it someone else's opinion?"

Josh's jaw clenched. "If you're implying I've been swayed by my wife or anyone else, then you don't know me. I'm asking you to clarify my assignment, because unless there's something else you want from me, I have found no evidence of drug cartels actively operating in Blakeley." Josh paused. "But having said that, I am curious about the landing strip behind Miller's house. It's hard to observe his comings and goings on it because it's on private property and not accessible by any public roads. Any attempt to surveil the landing strip would be impossible without being detected. So, if you want me to investigate Miller Blakeley officially, let's put that on the table and deal with it."

Larkin smiled, this time with more sincerity. "That's what I like about you, Josh. You'd never make a politician but you're a damn good lawman." Larkin punched a button on his desk phone and the assistant appeared almost instantaneously.

"Sir?"

"Take Mr. Hart to my private conference room and give him the Blakeley file to read." He turned to Josh. "You cannot copy or remove anything from that file, understood? And you will not discuss any of its contents with anyone, including Mrs. Hart and her insurance investigator friend. Is that clear?"

"Yes, sir."

Larkin's plastic smile returned. "Well, good. Now that we've cleared that up, I need to go to my meeting."

"Yes, sir," the assistant said. "They're waiting for you."

CHAPTER 15

The governor's private conference room was about ten feet square with a marble floor. The only furniture was a small table with four chairs, two on each side. No phones or other electronic equipment. No doubt this room had housed some interesting private conferences over the years.

The file in front of him was a typical reddish brown, heavy duty accordion file, often called a Redrope file after the original manufacturer. Josh glanced at his watch. It might take a while to go through this information, so he'd have to read fast.

After reviewing some of the papers in the file, Josh realized the task was shaping up to be easier than he thought, as much of the material was copies of newspaper clippings of Guinette Blakeley's suicide, which he had already seen, along with some other documents Josh had already seen. This wasn't a file maintained by an experienced administrative staffer. It looked more like someone just crammed notes in it.

Several articles explained Blakeley's history. The file also contained copies of reports showing how much money Miller Blakeley had contributed to Governor Larkin's various campaigns, which totaled nearly $10 million over a decade or more. Some of the funds appeared to have been passed through several channels before ending up in Larkin's coffers. No wonder he was so nervous about investigating his benefactor. But none of that was Josh's concern, other than how these transactions might affect Larkin's judgment.

After a few hours, Josh was getting tired of sitting in the uncomfortable chair and feeling claustrophobic in the small, windowless room. He quickly flipped through the remaining papers until one document caught his eye: a confidential report by an unnamed source, who appeared to be an investigator based on the tone and structure of the report. It suggested, without supporting evidence, that Miller had killed his wife and perhaps Abigail Sullivan as well. Much of the report referenced comments from unidentified sources.

Josh leaned back in the chair and exhaled deeply to clear his mind. He straightened himself in the chair and looked at the report again. This time it was Josh's own name that caught his attention. The report acknowledged what he had suspected all along: Josh's real assignment was to find out more about Miller Blakeley and whether he was involved in Guinette's death. The investigator acknowledged Miller was a drug addict and that the report wasn't intended to be a comprehensive investigation but a background check on Miller Blakeley.

Under different circumstances, Josh could almost feel sorry for Larkin. He was in a difficult situation. No doubt if the governor went after Miller, Miller would publicly let it be known he was a large financial backer of Larkin's two successful governor's campaigns. And knowing how politicians operate, there was probably more dirt swept under the rug.

At 5:00 p.m., the governor's assistant knocked on the door before opening it. "I'm sorry to disturb you, but I'm leaving now and I was instructed to secure that file before I left. Do you need to come back tomorrow?"

"No, I think I've seen enough." Josh tried to assume his best "aw shucks" demeanor. "I didn't see the investigator's name who compiled these reports. Is it in another file perhaps?"

The aide's smile was a clear message of *nice try*. "You'll have to ask Governor Larkin about that. Now if there's nothing else, I'll take that file." He leaned in and swooped the file up before Josh could respond. "And I'll show you out now."

· · ·

In times like these, Josh missed the camaraderie of fellow police officers he could talk to, share his thoughts with, and even ask for advice. What did Larkin expect Josh to do? On the two-lane state road back to Blakeley, Josh pulled off on the side of the road beside a small lake to clear his head. He glanced around for "No Trespassing" signs but saw none, so he walked down the short path to the water's edge.

Looking around for a small, flat rock, Josh tried to skip it across the water. But the rock sank instantly. He admired his brother and others who had mastered the feat. His brother had once told him finding the right rock was the key, but why was it he always found the right ones and Josh never did?

The sun was going down behind the trees that surrounded the small lake. Bits of the day's last rays of sunshine danced on the water. Maybe he and Enid should buy some land and move out, away from crooked politicians and murderous rich folks. Josh would be content living anywhere Enid was, but she needed more, and he wasn't going to force her into a life she didn't want. Her first husband, Cade Blackwell, had done that well enough.

Sometimes, when Enid didn't think Josh was looking, he could see sadness in her eyes. She was a smart woman and too young to idle her life away sitting on a porch by a lake. Besides, neither of them was independently wealthy. Repeatedly, she assured him she didn't miss working for the newspaper and reminded him that her determination to discover the truth had gotten her into some dangerous situations. But Josh knew she deserved a more enriching life than what he had given her.

While they had talked about his job as Blakeley's police chief being temporary, they were both ready to settle down and do meaningful work. If he had to give up law enforcement to make Enid happy, he would, because he knew she would make sacrifices for him. In fact, she had.

Today he learned Roo's suspicions about Miller Blakeley were possibly true. And he realized that if he proved Miller was guilty, he and Enid could no longer stay in Blakeley. They were already outsiders, and tarnishing the name of the founding family would push them further out. They'd have to sell the bookstore and move on. And Josh would likely have to leave law enforcement, at least in South Carolina, because Larkin had put him in an impossible situation. No one likes a snitch.

As the last rays of sunshine disappeared, Josh remembered Enid's response when another reporter asked why she had chosen that profession: "To find the truth."

As Josh walked up the dirt path back to his car, he began making plans to find out the truth about Miller Blakeley and to identify the confidential investigator who might help solve this case.

CHAPTER 16

By the time Josh got back to Blakeley, Enid had closed the shop, so he called to let her know he was coming in. He needed to make sure she was on board with his plan and its impact on their lives.

As he was putting his key in the lock, the door opened. Enid threw her arms around him. "What's wrong?" Josh asked. "You're white as a sheet."

"I'm fine. Come on in." She gestured upstairs. "We've got a visitor."

"Roo's back?"

"No, it's Timmy."

"You mean the kid from next door?" Josh locked the shop door behind him.

Enid nodded.

"Where is Petula?"

Before Enid could respond, Timmy was coming down the stairs. "Is she back yet?"

Enid kneeled down to be at eye level with the small boy. "No, but you're safe with us. I'm sure she'll be back soon."

"Is she tired of taking care of me?"

Enid blinked back tears as she hugged Timmy. "No, sweetheart. She loves you." She stood up. "Why don't you go back upstairs and go to sleep. I need to talk to Josh. Okay?"

Timmy nodded and headed back up the stairs.

Once he was out of sight, Josh pulled Enid to him and held her. "You're shaking," he said.

"Why would she leave him like that?"

"Sit down and tell me what you know. I'm sure there's some logical explanation."

Josh and Enid sat in the reading chairs. "I really don't know anything about Pet's disappearance, other than what Timmy told me. She told him to go upstairs to the apartment while she closed the shop and said she'd be up after she balanced the day's sales. He said he waited a long time before he went down to check on her. She was simply gone. He didn't know what to do, so he ran over here and rang the shop doorbell because I had already locked up."

"That doesn't sound like something she would do—just disappear and leave Timmy alone."

"I agree. After Timmy came over, I left him here and went next door to look for myself. The front door was locked but the back door was open. Her shop is as small as ours, so it didn't take long to look around. I even went upstairs to check their apartment. Nothing looked unusual upstairs or down. I found the shop keys and locked the back door. I was about to call you when you said you were coming home."

"Do you know any of her relatives or friends we could call?"

Enid shook her head. "I asked Timmy but he didn't know of any. Poor thing. First, his parents die, then his grandmother. And now he's living with someone who has vanished. I wonder about life sometimes. It can be cruelest to the most innocent."

Josh motioned for Enid to come over and sit on his lap. He buried his face in her hair and kissed her neck, as his mind raced, trying to connect all the dots. "I need to call the sheriff and get him to send a crime scene investigator out. That's one of the big disadvantages of being in a small town—no resources."

Enid stood up. "How did your meeting go?"

"It can wait." Josh's mind was racing as he calculated the unlikely coincidences piling up. What was going on in Blakeley?

CHAPTER 17

Josh leaned over to kiss Enid. "I'm going to the office. You've got a little while longer to sleep. Get some rest."

Enid sat up in bed. "I haven't slept much, and I doubt I can now."

"The sheriff's CSI will be going over everything shortly, so I want to be there. Will you be okay with Timmy?"

Enid frowned. "Just because I didn't want kids doesn't mean I'm afraid of them."

Josh smiled. "Well, I am. I guess you should keep him out of school today. We'll need to get a formal statement from him."

"I asked him about school. He said Pet was home-schooling him, so I'll try to get him set up."

"I imagine he could teach us both a thing or two about technology. Kids today are amazing when it comes to all that online stuff." He kissed her. "Call me if you need me." Before he walked out of the bedroom, he turned around. "Oh, I haven't made breakfast. Can you manage?"

"Of course. I can run a shop, cook meals, teach a kid, act as a substitute mom, and still be an amazing wife," Enid said as she laughed and threw her pillow at him. "Go on. I'll manage."

"One more thing. Do you know if Roo has turned in her report to authorize payment to Miller Blakeley?"

"I assume she has by now. Why do you ask?"

"Ask her to call me. Today. It's important. I'll fill you in later."

. . .

After Josh left, Enid fed Timmy a bowl of Cheerios. He didn't seem to like it and wasn't crazy about the almond milk either, but he ate like he was hungry.

"Tess will be here soon to drop off her goodies. You like those, don't you?"

"Yeah, especially the chocolate brownies."

Enid worried about giving him so much sugar, but now wasn't the time to focus on nutrition. "Do you want to do your school lessons today? It's okay if you'd rather not. I'm sure your instructor will understand."

"Miss Angie is fun. I'd like to go sign in."

Enid relaxed slightly. At least his classes would help take his mind off Pet's disappearance for a while. "I'm glad you're enjoying school. Education is important." Enid laughed at herself for sounding so parenty. "Do you need any help?"

Timmy jumped up. "I left my laptop at our house."

"You mean next door?"

Timmy nodded.

"Can you take classes from any computer?"

"I guess so."

"I'll set you up as a user on my laptop and then check about getting yours from next door." She hoped it wasn't covered in fingerprint dust by the time she retrieved it.

After making sure Timmy was able to sign in to his

classes, she called Josh. "Hey, sorry to bother you."

"You giving up already?"

"No, but I do need to get Timmy's laptop. Is that possible?"

"I'm next door now. Let me see if they've processed it, and I'll bring it over."

"Thanks. Oh, I need to get some kid-friendly food. Any chance you can drop off something he might want? Heart-healthy Cheerios didn't quite cut it this morning."

"You know I have to call social services about Timmy."

Enid's heart sank. Foster care was no place for a child. "Can't you wait a while? Maybe Pet will show up."

"I'll drop off a few things in a bit."

. . .

When Timmy was settled into his classes and Enid had opened the shop, she called Roo. "Hey, I know it's early but do you have a minute?"

"I've had my third cup of coffee so I'm good. Everything okay?"

"Well, yes and no. Josh wants you to call him right away."

"Oh, crap. Who complained about me this time?"

"No, nothing like that. Just call him. By the way, have you authorized payment to Miller Blakeley?"

"Well, yes and no. I verbally committed to sending in my final report, but, well, you know how busy I can get sometimes."

"In other words, you're stalling."

"Is that what the complaint was about? Who called Josh?

Was it the governor again?"

"Just call Josh. I don't need to be involved."

"Now you've got me worried. I'll call him."

CHAPTER 18

"Ready for a morning snack?" Enid waived a small plate with a chocolate brownie on it under Timmy's nose.

He held his fingers to his mouth. "Shhh." He pointed to the instructor on the screen.

"Sorry," she whispered. "I'll just leave this here." She put the plate on the small table where Timmy was using her laptop for classes. She left the room and shut the door behind her. At least she didn't have to worry about Timmy taking his schooling seriously.

The shop doorbell rang, so she went downstairs. Normally she wouldn't have locked the door during the day. After all, crime was nearly non-existent in Blakeley. At least it used to be. When she opened the door, a sheriff's deputy was standing there with a blue laptop in her hand covered in Star Wars stickers.

"Police Chief Hart said you wanted this. It's been dusted. I tried to clean all the powder off."

Enid reached for the laptop. "Thanks. I guess you can't tell me if there's any news on finding Pet."

The deputy smiled. "Chief Hart said you would quiz me, and that I shouldn't tell you anything. I read all your articles on those cases you reported on, so I know you're a good investigator. If you ever need a job, let us know."

"Thanks, but right now I'm just worried about Pet and Timmy."

"Yes, ma'am. I understand. We found all kinds of prints downstairs in the shop, which is understandable. Later today, we'll need to get the boy's prints to eliminate him from those we processed upstairs in the living area, although there's no indication of a crime scene upstairs."

"Did you find her car?"

"Yes, ma'am. It's parked right out back in her usual place." The deputy turned to leave. "Oh, I almost forgot. I've got some food in my car. I'll bring it in. I have two kids myself, about the boy's age, so I had an idea of what he might like."

"Wonderful. Thanks so much."

Enid took the laptop upstairs to Timmy and this time quietly left it on the futon where he had slept last night.

"It's okay. I'm working on my own now." He looked at the laptop and then back at Enid. "Did they find her?"

"Not yet, but everyone's looking." Enid paused. "Had Pet said anything about anyone bothering her or anyone strange hanging around the shop?"

Timmy appeared to be thinking then shook his head. "No, but she asked me if I'd mind living on the farm with her, because she might sell the shop."

"You mean she might retire?"

Timmy shrugged. "I guess. She just said she wanted to leave Blakeley. She seemed sad."

"Okay, thanks. I'll let you get back to your schoolwork now."

Enid sat down in one of the chairs to call Josh when he walked into the shop. "Hi, I'm glad you're here," she said. "I was just about to call you. Did Pet say anything to you about wanting to leave Blakeley?"

"No, why?"

"I don't have a good feeling about all of this. You don't think Timmy is in any danger, do you?"

"No, but that's why I haven't called child protective services yet. I figure he's safer here than anywhere else they could put him."

Enid smiled. "You're such a softie." She pulled him down by his shirt sleeve and kissed him. "And I love you for it." She paused. "Although I'm not sure about this mothering thing."

"You'll figure it out. And it's only temporary." Josh pointed upstairs. "Is he in a class now?"

"I was just up there earlier and he's working on his own. Why?"

"While I'm here, I thought I'd get a statement from him."

"Can you do that? I mean, he's just a kid."

"I can't use it in a court of law without him having a legally appointed guardian present, but I just want to talk to him. See if he knows anything. I hate he's had such a hard life at an early age. He deserves better."

· · ·

Josh tapped on the door to the small bedroom where Timmy was doing schoolwork. "Timmy, it's me. Josh. Can I come in?"

Timmy opened the door. "I'm done."

Josh followed him into the room and sat on the futon. "You like school?"

Timmy shrugged. "Yeah, it's fun, like when we study history or science. But I don't like math."

"I hear you. I didn't care for it myself when I was your age. Hey, do you mind if we chat a few minutes?"

Timmy shrugged. "Sure, I guess so."

"You're a smart guy, and I just wanted to know if there's anything else you may have thought of you can tell me about Pet. Like, Enid just mentioned that Pet wanted to leave Blakeley. Do you know why? Maybe something to do with the break-in at the apartment?"

"I don't know." His small face reflected his concern. "She said she was glad the box wasn't here."

"What box was she referring to?"

Timmy shrugged. "Something about a box Nana gave her." His eyes filled with tears. "I just want her to come home. When is she coming back?"

Josh motioned for Timmy to come over and sit beside him and then put his arm around the small shoulders that were carrying such a heavy load. "We're doing everything we can to find her. Until then, you can stay with us. Enid and I don't know much about being parents, but you can help us figure it out. Will you?"

Timmy wiped his nose with his shirt sleeve and nodded. "Thank you, Mr. Josh."

Josh pulled Timmy close. "It's just Josh, man. Just Josh."

As Josh walked downstairs, his cell phone rang. It was Roo. "Hi, Roo. I'm glad you called. I need to talk to you about something. Where are you working today, I mean what part of the state?"

Roo replied that she was working at her condo in

Charleston, doing some paperwork.

"Enid said you hadn't authorized payment yet. Is that right?"

Roo confirmed she had not but planned to turn the report in later that day.

"Don't. I need to talk to you first." They talked further and agreed Roo would come to Blakeley that afternoon since she couldn't stall the insurance company any longer. "Bring an air mattress. Your room has been rented to someone else."

• • •

Nearly an hour and a half later, Roo's vintage red pickup pulled up and parked in front of the small police station. When she walked in, Josh greeted her. "Let's go to the shop to talk. Just give me a minute to tell my officer where I'll be."

"I'll go on over there," Roo said. When she walked into the shop, she put her briefcase on the floor beside one of the chairs and reached her arms into the air to stretch her back.

"Stiff?"

"Oh, hey, Enid. Yeah, been spending a lot of time in the car lately." She motioned next door. "Josh said he'd be here in a minute. Do you know what this is all about?"

Enid motioned up the stairs. "I'll go up and get you a cup of coffee. Josh can fill you in."

"Got any more of those sweet buns Tess left? I missed lunch."

"Sure. I'll bring you a sandwich down too. We've got some homemade pimento cheese."

"Nothing says Southern food like homemade pimento cheese."

As Roo settled back into the chair, Josh came in. "Sorry to keep you waiting. And thanks for coming on short notice, but I wanted to talk to you before it was too late."

"Did you find something on Miller?"

"Maybe." He told Roo about his meeting with the governor and about the secret file. "You can't tell anyone about any of this."

"Then how can I stop the insurance company from paying him?"

"I'm going to write you a letter."

"A letter? And say what? That you agree my suspicions *may* be right? I don't think that will cut it."

"I'm going to say that based on confidential information I've received, I, as police chief of Blakeley, am investigating one of our citizens, Miller Blakeley, for the possible murder of his wife."

Roo leaned back in her chair. "Whoa. That's pretty serious, dude. Won't you get fired? Or is that your plan?"

"I think my days here are numbered anyway. I hate it for Enid, because—"

"Because you think I'd put keeping the shop over doing the right thing?"

Josh spun around. "I didn't see you."

Enid put a tray on the small table beside Roo. "I'll just leave this."

"No wait," Josh said. "I want you to hear this too." He

exhaled loudly, wringing his hands. "After my meeting with Larkin, I've been giving this whole matter a lot of thought. Investigating someone isn't quite the same as accusing them, and I don't have much to go on." He turned to Roo. "But I might buy you a little more time. And I do intend to investigate him fully. Otherwise, I'm no better than some of the dirty cops I've investigated."

Roo jumped from her seat and put her arms around Josh's neck. "I love you." She turned to Enid. "You know, in a sisterly kind of way." She sat down again. "Okay, so what's the game plan? I need to send something to the insurance company today."

Enid stepped forward. "I'll work with Josh to prepare a statement. We can say he's investigating the death of Guinette Blakeley and recommends that no payment be made at this time."

"Thanks," he said to Enid. Then to Roo, "I'll fax it to your contact at the insurance company. I'm sure this is all highly irregular, but this is a strange situation." Josh sighed. "And I need to go see Miller before he gets wind of all this from his friend the insurance agent."

CHAPTER 19

Anyone who had lived in Blakeley for more than a day knew where Miller and his late wife lived. "Mansion" was the word most often used to describe the almost five thousand square foot plantation-style house just at the edge of town. The original founder of the town, Miller's great-grandfather, had built it with the wealth he accumulated from his lumber business. He defended the house's size by insisting it was built for the writers of Blakeley, not for himself. To back up his claim, he hosted readings, signings, and other writing-related events there weekly. He often invited writers to use his home as a retreat when they were working on a book of poems, a novel, or any creative project.

As Josh walked under the sprawling two-story porch to the front door, he questioned whether he was doing the right thing by confronting Miller Blakeley, considering the fact he had no evidence and the mayor could fire him as a result.

Taking a second deep breath, Josh pressed the doorbell, and he heard the loud, melodic door chimes through the massive oak door. After no one responded, Josh rang the bell again. Almost immediately a middle-aged woman opened the door. "Sorry, I was in the kitchen. May I help you?"

Josh showed her his badge. "I'm the Blakeley police chief, and I'm here to see Miller Blakeley. Is he in?"

The woman surveyed Josh from head to toe. "Does he know you're coming?"

Josh smiled. "I doubt it. Would you please tell him I'm here."

She pulled the door open a little wider. "Come on in. You can wait in here." She motioned to a formally decorated room that reminded Josh of Southern funeral homes. The furniture was visibly worn in places, and the room had an air of neglect.

"Thanks." Josh sat in one of the damask-covered wing chairs, which smelled of dust.

Miller kept him waiting about ten minutes, which Josh assumed was Miller's way of exerting control over the situation. When Miller entered, Josh stood but didn't offer his hand. "Mr. Blakeley, thanks for seeing me." Josh sat back down while Miller continued standing.

"I'm in the middle of something I need to attend to. What's all this about?"

If Josh had expected small talk and civility, he wasn't going to get either. "You're a man of few words, so I will be too. Please sit."

Miller's frown signaled his contempt.

"I want to let you know I'm formally investigating the death of your wife." Josh studied Miller's face, which remained stoic.

Is that so? And what is your investigation based on?"

"I have some information from a confidential informant that I need to check out." Josh cleared his throat. "I'm not charging you with anything at this time. I'm merely checking out some information that has come to light. You can consider this a courtesy call."

Miller made a noise that sounded like a horse with colic grunting. "Courtesy, my ass." Miller stood up. "I loved Guinette. We had a near perfect marriage, which is why her suicide came as a total shock." Miller stood to leave but turned back to Josh who was still seated. "If this is all some kind of political bullshit, you will pay for your stupidity," he said pointing his finger at Josh. He stormed out of the room leaving Josh sitting alone.

When the housekeeper walked in, Josh rose from his chair. "I guess I'm not welcome here any longer."

Unexpectedly, the housekeeper laughed. "Good for you." She walked back out into the hallway and called over her shoulder. "Shut the door when you leave."

CHAPTER 20

Josh figured he would at least make it back to the shop be-
fore his phone rang, but he had barely gotten into his car.
When he looked at the phone screen, he tensed. Governor
Larkin.

"Chief Hart here."

"And this is *your boss* calling."

Technically, Josh worked for the mayor of Blakeley, a
part-time public servant who also owned the local phar-
macy. But he decided not to clarify that point with Larkin.
"Yes, sir, I am aware of our relationship. How can I help
you?"

"Well, you could start by not running off half-cocked and
threatening the town's most prominent citizen."

Josh took a deep breath and considered his response. "If
you're referring to my chat with Miller Blakeley, I never
threatened him. It was a courtesy call. I felt I owed him
that."

The governor made the same kind of colicky-horse noise
Miller had. Maybe that was something they taught powerful
men. "I don't think Miller saw it that way. And what gives
you the right to use information I gave you in confidence?"

Josh pulled over to the side of the road and stopped the
car. "With all due respect, Governor, I know you gave me
that information so I would do what no one else had the
balls to do. So let's not play that game. If you want to fire

me, go ahead. That'll free me to talk to the press and to state law enforcement. I've about had it with all the secrets and good ol' boy crap. If you want to fire me, now's the time. Otherwise, I've got a missing person to investigate."

"I'm not going to fire you. At least not today. But just try not to piss off any more prominent citizens." With that, the governor ended the call.

Josh threw his phone on the seat and ran his fingers through his dark mane. "Urgggh! I hate politics." When the phone rang again, Josh was tempted to ignore it. He chuckled to himself. *Maybe Larkin is calling back to apologize.* But it was Enid's face on the screen.

"Hey, what's up?" he asked.

"I can't find Timmy."

"What do you mean?"

"I mean he's missing," Enid said.

"Crap, I'm on my way back home now. Officer Holden is at the police station. Tell him."

"Already did. Please hurry."

. . .

When Josh pulled up in front of the bookshop to park, he barely got out before Enid ran out to see him. "I've looked everywhere. He was studying upstairs, and then he just wasn't there."

Josh waved his arms around in a sweeping motion. "It's broad daylight. I doubt anyone could have gotten to Timmy without being seen."

Officer Sam Holden walked up to Josh. "We've looked

everywhere. No stranger seen around here. I think the boy ran away."

"Ran away?" Enid said. "But why would he do that?"

Holden shrugged. "The back door to your shop was open."

"And his backpack is missing," Enid said.

"Let's spread out in that wooded area behind here and see if we can find anything," Josh said.

Holden nodded and began walking toward the back of the shop.

"I'll help," Enid said.

Within a few minutes, Josh had organized the search party.

"Hey, boss. Look at this." Holden was pointing to a piece of clothing on a branch. "Could that be his?"

Enid pushed Josh aside to look at it. "That's from the shirt he had on."

"Well, at least we know we're headed in the right direction," Josh said. "Keep looking. He's couldn't have gotten too far ahead of us."

For the next thirty minutes, the search party combed through every leaf pile and every possible place a small child could hide. No sign of Timmy.

"The highway's on the other side of these woods. I think he might have been headed that way," Josh said.

"But why would he run away?" Enid asked.

"Just keep looking," Josh said. "We can get answers later. I put in a request at the sheriff's office for bloodhounds, but I don't know how quickly they'll get here." He turned to the others. "Keep moving, guys. We've got to find him before dark." *Or before someone else does.*

• • •

Enid heard Roo's voice. "Enid, what's going on?"

"Over here."

Roo trotted over to where Enid was standing. "I've been tromping around in these woods trying to find you. Someone in town told me Timmy is missing."

Enid nodded. "They think he ran away."

"I'll help you look. Which way?"

Enid pointed. "We're searching this area to the left." She walked towards a thicket of bushes and undergrowth. "Surely he didn't go through that. Let's walk over this way." She headed over to the right where Josh was on his police radio.

"Copy that. I'll be right there."

Enid told Roo to stay where she was. "I'm going to find out what's happening."

"I'm going too."

"No, stay here," Enid said. Josh was walking back the other way when she caught up with him. "Are you leaving? What happened?"

"I put a missing child alert out on him, and one of the sheriff's deputies saw a kid matching his description."

"Where?"

"On the highway, hitching a ride."

CHAPTER 21

By the time Josh got back to his car, onto the road, and to the highway where the deputy reported the sighting, Timmy was sitting in the back of the patrol car eating a candy bar. "Hey, deputy . . ." Josh looked at the name tag on his uniform. "Deputy Johnson. I'm relieved to see him. Did you find out anything?"

"I thought you'd rather ask, so I just detained him."

Josh smiled and nodded. "Thanks." He walked over to the patrol car and got into the back seat with Timmy. "Hey, buddy. You gave us all a big scare. Why'd you run away like that?"

Timmy looked up at Josh with big brown eyes filled with tears. "I didn't run away. I was going to the farm."

"What farm? You mean Pet's farm? Where you like to feed the animals?"

Timmy nodded. "Why didn't you just tell us you wanted to go there, and we'd have taken you."

"I saw her."

Josh looked up at Deputy Johnson, who just shrugged. "Do you mean Pet?" he asked.

"No, Nana."

"Your grandmother?" Josh asked.

Timmy nodded. "She was at the farm."

Josh straightened in his seat. "Wait, I'm confused. You saw your grandmother at Pet's farm. Was it a dream?"

Timmy shrugged. "She was talking to me, and I shut my eyes and saw her. She was motioning for me to come."

Josh put his arm around Timmy. "I know you're scared and you miss your grandmother." Josh could only imagine how lonely and abandoned Timmy must feel, especially with Pet gone now too. "So I can see how you might think you saw her."

Timmy pulled away from Josh. "No. I saw her. I did." His eyes brimmed with tears again.

"Okay, buddy, I believe you. Why don't we just go to the farm? Would you like to do that?"

Timmy nodded.

Josh got out of the patrol car and called Officer Holden. "I've got Timmy. Tell Enid he's fine. We'll be back there in a little while. I'm taking him to Pet's farm. Can you find the address and let me know where it is?"

Holden replied they had found that information in one of Pet's files in her office at the shop. He put Josh on hold and then came back in a few minutes with the address.

Josh got out and held out his hand to Timmy. "Come on to my car. You can sit up front with me. We're going to the farm."

. . .

Nearly an hour later, Josh and Timmy were close to the farm, according to the GPS coordinates. As they approached the dirt drive leading up to the house, a car passed them at a high rate of speed. Had it come from the farm? Josh couldn't be sure. It was getting dark and there was no lighting in the area at all. And his attention had been on find-ing the place.

Josh turned onto the narrow dirt road leading from the highway to the old farmhouse. After he parked, he got two LED flashlights from his trunk and handed one to Timmy. "Here's one for you. Don't want you to trip on anything." Josh glanced around. "Anyone stay here to care for the place?"

"Nellie and Will. But they go home at night."

"Do you know their last names?"

Timmy shook his head.

"Do you know where they live?"

Timmy shook his head again. "A cabin somewhere. That's all I know."

"Okay, so let's see what we can find here." Not that he had any idea what they were looking for. "Which way?"

Timmy looked around and then pointed. "That way."

"The barn?"

Timmy nodded. "That's where Nana was."

"Okay, but stay behind me." Josh walked toward the barn, hoping if they searched the area and found nothing Timmy would be satisfied. Josh kneeled down to talk to him. "You understand your grandmother is in heaven, right?"

"I know. But she talks to me all the time."

Josh stood up. "Okay, then let's keep going."

When they got to the barn, Josh noticed the door was partially open. "You stay here. I'll go inside." Josh aimed his flashlight into the dark building and walked inside, glancing over his shoulder to make sure Timmy had stayed outside.

The inside of the barn smelled musty, not like the sweet

hay smell Josh remembered from his childhood. He checked the empty horse stalls but saw nothing unusual. A wooden ladder led to the hayloft, but because Josh didn't like heights or trust ladders, he decided to stay on the ground. As he took one last glance around, he heard a noise. Not a scuffling noise like barn rats make. It was more like a moan.

Assuming it was a hurt animal, Josh began talking in a soothing voice. "It's okay. Let me know where you are so we can help you."

Another moan. This time it was more distinct.

Out of the corner of his eye, Josh saw Timmy. "No, go back outside." But Timmy kept walking and went straight to the ladder. "No, don't go up there. You might fall."

Ignoring Josh, Timmy scampered up the ladder much quicker than Josh ever could have. From the top of the hayloft, Timmy called out, "She's here."

Pushing his fears aside, Josh gingerly climbed up the ladder. Timmy was holding Pet's hand. The rest of her body was partially covered in straw.

"Stand back, Timmy." Josh brushed the straw away and checked her pulse. She was barely alive. "Just lie still," he said to Pet. "We'll get you some help." Josh radioed his dispatcher and gave her the information.

Timmy was still holding Pet's hand. "Please wake up," he murmured to her.

Josh put his hand on the boy's shoulder. "How did you know she was here?"

"I heard her."

"No, I mean when we were back at the bookshop. You said your grandmother told you to come here."

Timmy shrugged.

Josh put his arm around Timmy. "It's alright. We'll figure all this out later. For now, let's get her to the hospital."

CHAPTER 22

It took nearly thirty minutes for the county ambulance to arrive. During that time, Timmy never left Pet's side. The EMTs checked her carefully before strapping her onto a stretcher and lowering her down.

"Will she make it?" Josh asked one of the EMTs when they were out of earshot from Timmy.

"Hard to say, sir. She's barely got a pulse. We'll do the best we can."

Josh nodded and went back inside the barn to get Timmy, but he was already headed toward Josh. "Is Pet going to die too?"

"I hope not, buddy," Josh said. "You know, you probably saved her life."

Timmy smiled slightly.

On the ride back to the bookstore, Josh called Enid and told her they had found Pet. When she asked him how they knew to look at the farm, he told her they'd talk about it later and asked her to put a fresh pot of coffee on. He needed something stronger but wanted to keep a clear head. He imagined someone reading his report and saying, "Yeah, right." He'd have to figure out how to report Timmy's uncanny behavior.

After the call ended, Josh asked Timmy, "Does your grandmother talk to you a lot?"

"You mean since she went to heaven?"

Josh smiled. "Yes."

"Not a lot. She mostly comes to see me when I'm scared. She tells me everything will be alright."

"I'm glad." Although Josh wasn't sure he meant it. "Why don't you lie back and take a nap. You're probably pretty tired."

Timmy laid his head back against the seat. In a few minutes, Josh heard the steady, quiet breathing of a child sleeping.

. . .

Enid helped Timmy get into his pajamas and into bed and then joined Josh downstairs so they wouldn't disturb Timmy. "I still can't believe you found Pet."

"I just realized something. Where's Roo? I thought she was going to sleep on the air mattress."

"She was summoned to the insurance company tomorrow, so she went back to Charleston for the night."

"I hope my visit to Miller Blakeley doesn't get her fired."

"Me too." Enid poured Josh a cup of coffee. "I made you a sandwich. Figured you probably missed lunch today."

Josh smiled. "Now that you mention it, I guess I did." He ate about half the sandwich and laid the rest back on the plate. "I don't know how to explain what happened today." Josh took several sips of black coffee. "A county deputy spotted Timmy on the highway. He was trying to get to Pet's farm."

"Why was that?"

"This is where it gets weird. He claims his grandmother

told him to go there."

"You mean Abigail Sullivan? Who's dead?"

Josh smiled. "Yep, that's the one. Anyway, he says she talks to him a lot."

"Did she tell him why to go there?"

"No, I don't think so. When we got there, it was dark. I asked Timmy where he wanted to go, and he took me to the barn. I was looking around, heard a noise, and then Timmy came in and went straight up to the hayloft. That's where we found Pet. She was barely alive."

Enid poured herself a cup of coffee. "That's bizarre. He couldn't possibly have known she was there. Maybe there's some other explanation."

"If there is, I'd love to hear it. My report is going to be the joke of the century."

"I think we need to get him checked out. Psychologically, I mean. The poor kid has been through so much. First his grandmother dies, and he has to go live with Pet, whom he barely knew. And then she disappears. It's more than one child should have to bear. I want to make sure he gets the emotional support he needs."

Josh motioned for Enid to sit on his lap. "I need support too, you know. I might be traumatized from being away from you so much."

Enid leaned in and kissed him. "Poor baby. I'll take care of you tonight, but tomorrow I'm going to find someone to talk to Timmy."

CHAPTER 23

Josh had left early for work and Enid was explaining to Timmy where they were going. "Pet is still in the hospital and they're taking good care of her. As soon as she can have visitors, I'll take you to see her." Enid said another silent prayer for Pet. She had been stabbed and left for dead in the hayloft. The odds of a complete recovery were slim, but the doctors held out hope she might surprise them.

"Today we're going to see a lady who loves talking to children your age. She wants you to tell her about your grandmother talking to you. Will you talk to her when we get there?"

Timmy's face was expressionless. "Why does she want to know?"

"Because your story is so interesting. Will you talk with her?"

Timmy shrugged. "I guess so."

"Okay, let's go then."

Nearly two hours later, Enid held onto Timmy's hand as they walked down the sidewalk in a historic section of Columbia called Elmwood Park, a neighborhood in the downtown area. The houses were old with big porches. Most had been beautifully renovated, and the yards were well kept. Residents included an eclectic mixture of business professionals, families, and artistic-leaning residents who appreciated the convenient location and neighborhood friendliness.

Dr. Sims, a retired child psychologist, lived in a beautiful bungalow with a wrap-around porch. A "Yard of the Month" sign was proudly displayed near the front steps.

Enid rang the doorbell, which was much louder than any she had ever heard, and almost immediately the front door opened. An older woman opened the door. "Ah, you must be Timmy." She leaned over to make eye contact and to extend her hand. "I'm Dr. Sims. Come on in."

Enid and Timmy followed her inside to the small living room. "Have a seat here, Timmy. This is a special chair. It belonged to my daughter when she was about your age." The chair was a slightly smaller version of a traditional wing chair. It was upholstered in denim fabric with the same feel as well-worn jeans.

Dr. Sims pulled up a small stool and sat near Timmy. "Would it be alright if Ms. Blackwell stayed in here with us, or would you rather talk to me alone?"

Timmy looked at Enid and nodded. "She can stay."

"Excellent. Now before we get started, I just need to talk to Ms. Blackwell about a few things. I understand you like UFOs and ghost stories. Is that right?"

Timmy nodded.

Dr. Sims handed him a small hardcover book. "This book is about ghosts in Columbia. Why don't you read it? One of them is in a house just down the street."

Timmy smiled as he took the book from her.

Dr. Sims nodded for Enid to follow her to a small room at the back of the house that was furnished as an office. "I just need to reiterate what we talked about earlier. I'm seeing

Timmy as a favor to Jack Johnson. He said you used to work for his newspaper and that you called asking if he knew someone who could see Timmy unofficially."

"Yes, I called him last night." Enid had considered contacting Karla, an empath she had worked with when searching for Roo's missing aunt. But Karla was elusive and liked to stay in the shadows, unreachable. Even if she could have located Karla, her approach might be more than Timmy could handle right now.

"Jack's good people, and I owe him for helping me on a personal matter. As you know, I'm retired, so this is an off-the-books visit, as you requested. I'm just a friend helping a friend. If I think Timmy needs additional counseling, I'll refer you to a child psychologist."

Enid nodded. "Of course."

"By the way, how is the woman who was attacked?"

Enid gave her an update on Pet's condition.

"We just need to make sure Timmy is . . . we just need to understand what happened."

Dr. Sims smiled. "You want to know if he's crazy or psychic. Is that about it?"

Enid nodded. "Yes, something like that."

"Alright then, let's go talk to Timmy. I expect you to remain silent unless I invite you into the conversation."

"Understood."

When they returned to the living room, Timmy was engrossed in the book. "Can we go see this house?" He pointed to an illustration of the house down the street.

Dr. Sims laughed. "Maybe we can walk past it after we finish. How about that?"

Timmy smiled and nodded his head.

"And you can sit over there." Dr. Sims directed Enid to an antique wooden, Windsor-style chair in the corner. The dark stain was worn off the seat and both arms. Dr. Sims sat on the small stool in front of Timmy. "Tell me about your grandmother and how she talks to you."

Timmy looked up at the ceiling as though he was searching for an answer. "She comes to see me at night sometimes."

"While you're asleep?"

"No. Well, maybe. I'm almost asleep sometimes when she comes."

"When she told you to go to the farm, what else did she say?"

Timmy shrugged. "I don't remember anything else."

"Did she tell you Pet would be there?"

Timmy was silent for a moment. "No, I don't think so."

"Did you know Pet would be there?"

Timmy looked puzzled. "I thought she might be there feeding the animals."

"Why did you go to the highway by yourself instead of asking someone to take you?"

Timmy glanced over at Enid, who smiled and nodded. "I knew everybody was busy, and I had to go. Nana told me to go there." Timmy's eyes filled with tears.

"It's okay, Timmy. You saved Pet's life so you're not in any trouble. We all appreciate your help." Dr. Sims paused. "So when you got there, the police chief told you to stay outside, but you went into the barn where Chief Hart was. What made you do that?"

Timmy shrugged. "I wanted to see if Betsy was in there."

"Who is Betsy?"

"She's a little goat. She lives on the farm."

Dr. Sims smiled. "Ah, I see. Then what happened? After you went into the barn?"

"I heard something up there." He pointed up with his finger.

"You heard Pet?"

Timmy nodded. "Can you tell them to let me see her?"

"She needs to get a little stronger first. Let's just keep sending her our healing thoughts, okay?"

Timmy nodded and wiped his eyes with the sleeve of his shirt.

"Is there anything else you can tell me about these visits from your grandmother? Do you hear words or just know what she's trying to tell you?"

"I mostly just know. Will she keep coming to see me?"

Dr. Sims gently tapped Timmy's chest. "She'll always be right there in your heart. Anytime you need her. If she doesn't talk to you, it's because she knows you're doing just fine on your own. But you can talk to her anytime. I know she'd like that. You're a brave, determined young man, and I know she's very proud of you. She wants you to be happy. Can you do that for her?"

Tears ran down Timmy's cheeks. "I'll try." Without warning, he leaned over and hugged Dr. Sims, as the sobs shook his small body.

Dr. Sims handed Timmy a tissue and then turned to Enid. "I'll call you later." She smiled at Timmy. "Now let's go walk past the ghost house. Who knows what we might see."

CHAPTER 24

Like most people, Josh hated hospitals—the smell, the suffering. But it was part of the job, and he was in such places more often than he liked. He walked to the nurse's station and showed her his badge. "I need to see—"

The nurse smiled. "I know why you're here, Chief Hart. Follow me." Josh followed her down the long, white corridor. "You need to keep it short. She's weak and tires easily. And please try not to upset her. I know you have your job to do, but I have mine."

"Yes, ma'am."

A sheriff's deputy sat outside one of the rooms. He stood when he saw Josh. "Chief," he said in acknowledgment.

"Deputy, if you need to take a break, now's the time. I'll be with her for a little while."

"A *very* little while," the nurse said. She walked into the room ahead of Josh. "Miss Petula, a nice police officer is here to talk with you. Do you feel like it?"

Pet nodded slightly, as the nurse patted her arm. "When you get tired, push your call button, and I'll come rescue you." The nurse glanced at Josh before she left the room.

Josh pulled a small chair up beside the bed. "Pet, do you remember me?"

She managed a small smile. "Of course. I didn't hit my head." Her voice wavered, and she spoke so softly Josh could barely hear her.

"I don't want to upset you, but I'd like to ask a few questions."

Pet nodded. "Is Timmy . . . is he okay?"

"Yes, he's fine. Enid's taking good care of him. What do you remember about the attack?"

Pet's hand was shaking. "I went to take the trash out back. Someone grabbed me. Then I remember being in a car."

"Did they say anything that you can remember?"

She grasped her shaking hand with her other one and turned her head away from Josh, tears streaming down her cheeks. "One of them asked me if I had any of Abigail's records."

"How many men were there?"

"Two. At least I think so. They put something over my head. I couldn't see but I heard two different voices."

"And *do* you have any of her records?"

"Over the years, she's left several things at the farm for me to keep. She used to laugh and say she owed me a storage fee. But I had all that space and didn't mind at all. She left dozens of boxes with me, but she said they were just memories. That's what she called them. Memories to share with Timmy when he was older."

"So when the men grabbed you, they took you to the farm?"

"Yes, I guess so." Pet cried softly and Josh handed her a tissue from the small bedside table. "I'm sorry, it's all fuzzy now. I can't remember much."

About that time, the nurse walked in. "Okay, Miss Petula. I think you've had enough visiting today. You need to rest."

The nurse glanced at the tissues on the bed and then at Josh. "We don't want you upset, now do we?"

· · ·

Not long after Enid and Timmy got back to the shop, her cellphone rang. "Timmy, I'm going upstairs to take this call. You stay here. Okay?" She recognized the number.

Timmy headed straight for the section of books on ghosts, although it contained only a few books and he had read them all.

"Hello, Dr. Sims," Enid said as she walked up the stairs.

"I'd like to discuss my visit with Timmy this morning if you have a few minutes. How is Petula?

"I think she's awake now."

"Thank goodness. I don't know her, but I'm happy for Timmy's sake. He's such a wonderful boy. Can you talk now?"

"Sure. Timmy's downstairs reading ghost books."

"Does that concern you?" Dr. Sims asked.

"I'm not sure. He seems to be obsessed with ghosts—and UFOs."

"Kids are naturally curious, and Timmy's a bright child. I remember when I was about his age, I read all the ghost stories I could find. So I wouldn't worry at this point."

"But what about his grandmother, Abigail, talking to him?"

"There's been a lot of research conducted on children's encounters with supernatural beings. It's more common than you might expect. Kids have a natural openness to such things, whereas we adults rationalize and dismiss anything we can't explain."

Enid felt a trickle of cold sweat running down her spine. "Are you saying ghosts are real and that Abigail really did talk to Timmy?"

Dr. Sims laughed softly. "I'm saying anything is possible. When I was talking with Timmy this morning, he seemed to take comfort in knowing his grandmother was with him. Is that the impression you get?"

"Yes, I'd agree with that. Do you think he's imagining she's around so he'll feel safe?"

"Whether it's real or imagined isn't important, at least not now. If Timmy isn't distressed by his grandmother's ghost, then we shouldn't be either. I'm guessing these visits from her will diminish once he's more settled into a routine and feels safe again. But maybe she is watching over him. I'm just glad to know he's staying with you and Chief Hart."

"It's only temporary."

"Of course."

"So is there anything we need to do to help Timmy?"

"Just do what you're doing now. Make him feel as safe and secure as possible. He needs to know you're there for him. I'll check in with you in a week or so, but you can call me if you have any questions. I assume you know this, but you need to file a request to become Timmy's guardian, even if a temporary one. Not reporting this situation is illegal and could jeopardize Timmy's future. If you have a pen and paper, I can give you the number of who you need to contact."

Enid took down the information. "I'll talk to Josh about applying. How much do I owe—?"

"I told you, I'm not a practicing psychologist any longer. Just make a small donation to your favorite charity and we're even. Better yet, buy Timmy another ghost book."

CHAPTER 25

When Roo arrived at the insurance office in Charleston, her stomach was in knots. She'd likely be fired and maybe worse—blackballed by the company so she couldn't work again as an insurance investigator. Maybe if she begged forgiveness, she could keep her job. But then she'd have to ignore her basic instincts, ignore the fact that Miller Blakeley likely killed his wife and her personal assistant.

And that whole business of Pet being abducted. What was that about? As these thoughts were bouncing around in her head, a woman approached her. "They're ready for you. Follow me."

They? Roo followed the woman down the long marble hallway, her high heels making a tapping noise with each step. Suddenly, the woman stopped and motioned for Roo to go into a large conference room. The bottom half of the wall was wood paneling and the top half was opaque glass, so that no one could see anything inside other than shadows of people.

Roo jumped slightly when the door closed behind her.

"Have a seat, Ms. Murray." A man Roo didn't recognize motioned for her to sit across the table from him. "I'm the regional vice president of claims for Foster Insurance. I don't believe we've had the pleasure of meeting." He stared at Roo and then flipped through a file on the table. It didn't take a genius to figure out which file he had. "I don't normally get involved in investigations like these, but our sales vice president, Nathan Adams, has filed a complaint against us for the delay in settling."

The man Roo routinely reported to was at the end of the table and appeared to be avoiding eye contact with her, so she ignored him as well. "A pleasure to meet you, as well, Mr. Roberts." He didn't express surprise that she knew his name, but she had seen his signature in files many times, so she felt like she knew him.

The man rested his arms on the table and leaned forward. "Now that we have those niceties out of the way, I imagine you'd appreciate our getting to the point."

"Yes, sir." She decided to follow courtroom rules: don't volunteer anything and just answer the questions truthfully.

"What can you tell us about the Miller Blakeley claim?"

Roo pointed to the folder. "I believe it's all in there, and I imagine you've read my reports. Do you have the one I just sent in?" She tried to maintain an I'm-just-doing-my-job demeanor.

Roberts leaned back in his chair. "You have a good reputation around here. While you haven't done much work for us, I'm familiar with some of the cases you've investigated." He paused. "But this one puzzles me. After all, Mr. Blakeley is perhaps the most prominent citizen in a town named after his family." Roberts smiled. "I'm sure you realize how delicate this situation is."

Roo tried to focus on lowering her racing heartbeat. "Yes, sir. I appreciate the dilemma my reports have put your insurance company in." She took another breath. "But I believe Miller Blakeley murdered two people, his wife and his wife's assistant." The air in the room was suddenly sucked out and Roo felt lightheaded. "I cannot alter my reports."

"But you also can't prove he did it, now can you?" Roberts reminded Roo of her economics professor, the one who yelled at his students a lot and took pleasure in failing them.

"As I said in my last report, Police Chief Joshua Hart has opened an investigation into these deaths, which were initially reported as a suicide and an accident."

Roberts continued to stare at her. To break the uncomfortable silence, Roo continued. "I know you have sixty days to pay the claim or deny it once all the documentation is received. But I also know that the insurance carrier can delay payment until the beneficiary is cleared of any wrongdoing."

Roberts leaned back in his chair and smiled. "I was told you wouldn't back down." He leaned forward and slammed the file shut. Roo couldn't help but jump slightly. "I'm delaying payment for another sixty days. However, our sales department, including Andy Pratt and his boss, won't be happy with me. Hard to sell insurance, especially in a small town, when a company gets a reputation for delaying settlement." His eyes bored into Roo. "But under the circumstances, I have no choice." The tension in the room was palpable. "In the meantime, I expect you to send regular reports, keeping us apprised of Chief Hart's investigation." When Roo started to speak, Roberts held up his hand to stop her. "I realize you will have only limited access to this information but do your best. Understand?"

"Yes, sir, and—" Before she could finish, Roberts stood up, file in hand, and stormed out of the room.

...

After leaving the meeting, Roo decided to drive to Blakeley. She needed to update Josh and hopefully convince him to keep her informed as much as he could. She didn't feel any loyalty to the insurance company, but she'd like to keep her reputation intact if possible. She had sixty days before Roberts would likely decide to pay Miller Blakeley's claim for his wife's insurance policy.

There was no insurance claim on Abigail Sullivan, so Roo had no right to ask Josh about that investigation. But Roo was convinced the two deaths were intertwined. Perhaps if they could prove Sullivan's death was not an accident, they could leverage that information into more time to delay payment.

Roo realized the strange noise she heard was her stomach growling in hunger. She hadn't eaten, so she pulled off at the next exit to look for a Mexican restaurant that was supposed to be nearby. She turned right and went a couple of miles without seeing it, so she opted to stop at a gas station and buy a refrigerated egg salad sandwich and a carton of milk. Not the tastiest lunch she'd ever had, but it served its purpose.

Once she was on the road again, she called Enid to let her know she was coming. When Enid reminded her that Timmy was still staying with them, Roo offered to sleep on the floor but was assured they could work something out.

The drive to Blakeley gave Roo a chance to think about Abigail Sullivan and why Miller Blakeley might want her dead.

CHAPTER 26

The Blakeley Police Department was in a small building but it was big enough for their staff of three: Josh, his only police officer, and a dispatcher. On the rare occasions when the Blakeley PD needed help, they called on the county sheriff for assistance. The sheriff repeatedly asked why Blakeley needed its own police department, and the mayor always gave the same response: the town prided itself on being self-sufficient.

Now Josh had a decision to make. If he called in the South Carolina Law Enforcement Division, SLED, to help with the case or turned it over to the sheriff's office, the case would be out of his hands. Josh was reasonably sure the sheriff would simply close the case because he and Miller Blakeley were hunting buddies. A picture of the sheriff and Miller was proudly displayed in the sheriff's office, with them standing over an eight-point buck. Even though Josh had grown up in a hunting family, they hunted for food. Josh didn't see the point in killing such magnificent animals purely for sport.

SLED would be the better choice to help with the case, but they may consider the evidence too sparse to justify taking it on. And they may get political pressure from Governor Larkin to drop it.

Josh also accepted the fact he just wasn't ready to let go. He owed Timmy and Pet the most thorough investigation he could conduct. Turning it over to another law enforcement agency would be admitting defeat and surrendering control. But he also knew he'd have to move fast and reconsider his position if he couldn't prove something soon.

The nurse at the hospital had agreed to let Josh return later that day to continue his questions. Josh had checked in with the dispatcher and tried to make an appointment to see the Blakeley mayor before he went to see Pet, but the mayor was at a luncheon.

On the drive back to the hospital, Josh reflected on the events leading up to this point. It all began with Guinette Blakeley's alleged suicide. The timing was suspicious since it occurred just after the two-year suicide waiting period had expired. And the amount of the insurance policy provided sufficient motive. But this information wasn't evidence, only a suspicion. And then Abigail Sullivan allegedly fell down the steps and broke her neck, dying almost instantly. She had access to the Blakeley family secrets, as well as Guinette's personal financial records and other information. And now Abigail's best friend, Pet, who is also caring for Abigail's grandson, was the victim of a break-in and then an abduction. As Roo suspected all along, these events appeared to be connected. But how could he prove it?

• • •

After getting the same warning from the nurse she gave previously, Josh agreed not to upset Pet. He sat by her hospital bed.

"I'm sorry you got thrown out before," Pet said. "It's

just that—"

"You don't have to apologize. I know this is all very stressful for you. Are you up for a few more questions?"

Pet nodded.

"Do you know where Abigail put the boxes on your farm?"

"She never said exactly what was in them or where she put them. I assume in one of the empty bedrooms, a closet, or somewhere like that." Pet slowly shook her head. "Poor Abigail, she didn't realize she made me a target."

"Did she tell you anything about Guinette's personal situation, you know, with Miller?" Josh asked.

"Can you give me a sip of water first?"

Josh removed the paper wrap from a straw and put it in a glass with some water from the Styrofoam pitcher.

Pet drank several swallows before she handed the glass back to him. "I know she shouldn't have told me about their personal affairs, but Guinette needed to talk to someone. I was all she had. And you're the only person I've told this to."

"I'm not here to judge you or Guinette, but you need to tell me anything that might help this investigation. Understand?"

Pet nodded. "Guinette trusted Abigail with all her finances and told her most everything about her personal matters, including the fact that Miller had withdrawn funds from her personal checking account without permission."

"So the Blakeleys kept separate accounts?"

Pet nodded. "Guinette inherited a large sum of money from her father's estate. He was a successful tobacco farmer and a savvy stock investor. Abigail said Guinette often wondered if Miller had married her for her bank account. They had no children, and Guinette spent little money on herself, so the account grew to nearly $10 million."

Josh sat back in his chair. "That's some serious money."

Pet nodded. "She said she was going to leave most of it to charitable organizations. But I don't think Miller knew that."

"But why did Miller need his wife's money? Isn't he wealthy on his own?"

"He was at one time. According to Guinette, Miller made some bad investments. And then to make matters worse, he got shot accidentally on one of the hunting weekends with a bunch of his buddies. One of them had too much to drink and shot Blakeley thinking he was a deer. During his recovery, Miller got hooked on pain pills. Our local dentist made sure he never ran out."

"So did Abigail think he was spending his money on drugs?"

"Yes, but Guinette also suspected Miller of selling drugs. He was desperate to restore his own wealth, and he didn't really have a profession, thanks to his inheritance. So he took an unexplained trip to Mexico, and then bought a small plane and began meeting with what Guinette described as 'strange low-life men' late at night."

"I saw a small landing strip on their property when I was there."

"He had that built when he bought the plane. Guinette confronted Miller about the planes and strange visitors coming and going. When she did, he slapped her in the face."

Pet shook her head. "Abigail said things went downhill from there."

"What did she mean?"

"Miller began staying away for days. Nobody knew where he was. One night, two armed men showed up at the house demanding to see Miller. When Guinette told them she had no idea where he was, they threatened to burn the house down."

"Why didn't she move out or call us?"

Pet smiled slightly. "I think you know the answer. She didn't know if you were in cahoots with Miller too. You were fairly new in town, and she felt like she had nowhere to turn."

"Except to Abigail," Josh said.

Pet nodded. "And then Guinette died. She didn't kill herself. Abigail was sure of it. She was named as executor of Guinette's estate, and Miller began quizzing her about where the money was going. That's about the time Abigail asked me if I would take care of Timmy if anything happened to her. Of course, I said yes. But I honestly thought nothing of it. After all, Abigail had no close relatives, so it made sense to me that she would have a contingency plan." Pet lowered her head. "I should have come to you myself, but I had no idea she was in danger. When she died, I went straight to her house to look for her personal papers. You know, as her executor. But I didn't find anything." She paused. "I thought that was strange because Abigail kept meticulous notes and records—on everything."

"What do you think happened to her papers?"

"I thought maybe someone had taken them, but then

when I was . . ." Her voice trailed off. "When I was taken, I began wondering who had her files." She looked up and made eye contact with Josh. "You know, she always kept a journal. I know she wanted Timmy to have them."

"What did she put in her journals?"

"Everything. It's how she processed and made sense of the world around her, especially Blakeley."

"Did anyone else know about these journals?"

"Guinette did. And one other person. Miller knew Abigail kept journals about everything."

CHAPTER 27

When Roo arrived in Blakeley, she went straight to the police station to confront Josh. No point in beating around the bush. Josh was sitting at his desk, going through a file when Roo walked into the station. "Hey, Josh. What's up."

"As if you didn't know." Josh stood and gave her a hug. "Enid told me you were coming back to town so I expected you'd stop by." He motioned to a metal chair in front of his desk. "Please. Have a seat."

Roo threw her worn briefcase on the floor. "Before you start, I *know* there are things you can't tell me. So just fill in the blanks where you can."

"Actually, I need you to help me. I'd like to see your investigation notes if you're willing to share them."

"Well, that was unexpected. What are you looking for exactly?"

"I'm not really sure." Josh explained his dilemma about going to SLED or the county sheriff."

"So you want to do this on your own? You sure that's a good idea?"

Josh laughed. "No. In fact, I'm pretty sure it's a terrible idea. But before I involve another law enforcement agency that will likely take over, I want to make sure I have enough information to keep them from sweeping it under the rug."

"I doubt my company would allow me to give you access to my file without a warrant. But seeing as how I have a personal interest in seeing that scumbag hang, I might be willing to let you take a peek and ask me any questions." She laughed. "Imagine that, Chief Joshua Hart needs my help."

"When I learned you were trying to deny life insurance payments to Miller, I didn't understand what made you so suspicious of him."

"The timing of it, for one thing. His wife died just after the suicide clause period ended. Then when his wife's assistant allegedly fell down the steps, I just knew he was behind both deaths." She waved her arms in the air for emphasis. "I can't prove it. I just know it."

"Why don't you go over to the shop with Enid." Josh glanced at Roo's briefcase and smiled. "If you happen to forget and leave something behind, I'll make sure you get it back."

Roo took her file on Miller Blakeley and laid it on Josh's desk. "Yes, I'd appreciate your returning anything I might *accidentally* leave behind. By the way, is there a place around here where I can get a room? I know Timmy is still with you, so I think it would be easier on all of us if I found a place. Besides, the company is paying for it."

"I think Pet would be glad for you to stay at her place. She's still in the hospital but I'll run by there and confirm it's alright with her."

"That'd be great. Thanks."

· · ·

After Roo left, Josh settled down at his desk to look at Roo's investigation file. Unfortunately, there wasn't anything in it that he didn't already know. Not that he was one to dismiss gut feelings, but it appeared Roo had based her conclusions on some facts and a lot of gut. Even though he had come to respect Roo's investigative skills, as well as her instincts, he wasn't surprised the insurance carrier was uncomfortable denying payment with what she had.

He decided the best plan was to go back to everyone Roo had talked to, which wasn't that many people, and ask them for more details. As a law enforcement officer, he hoped they would be more forthcoming with him, but the opposite could also be true.

Not that he had any firm goals. Handling assignments for the governor wasn't what he had planned as a career path. But if it meant bringing bad guys to justice, he could stomach it. For a while, at least. But did he really want to be a sheriff again? No law enforcement path he could imagine was free of politics. He had to accept that fact. And he was fairly certain his and Enid's future wasn't in Blakeley. They were outsiders and given the town's origins, they would never be recognized as otherwise. Once the mayor, town council, and citizens of Blakeley found out he was there primarily to find dirt on their founding family, he and Enid would be outcasts. He was sure of it. No matter what Miller Blakeley might have done, he was a big part of the town's history and admired by many. The majority of Blakeley's citizens would not accept that Miller was guilty, regardless of what proof Josh might produce.

But enough worrying for now. He told the dispatcher he was going to see Andy Pratt, the insurance agent who sold the life policy on Guinette Blakeley.

Since the insurance office was just down the street, he was there in less than ten minutes. A young woman with long blond hair seated at the reception desk greeted him. "Hi, how can we help you, Chief Hart?"

"I'm here to see Andy. Is he in?"

"He is, but he has someone in his office. Would you like to wait? He should be finishing up soon." She leaned forward and whispered. "It's a *big* life policy." She finished with a girlish giggle. "Andy will be happy."

"You mean because of his commission?"

The girl looked surprised. "Well, yeah. I mean, he's under a lot of pressure. I think it stresses him out some." Another award-winning smile. Josh figured her as an ex-beauty queen.

"So does Andy write for different companies?"

She shrugged. "Well, yeah, I mean he represents a lot of insurance companies, but most of his business is with one company. I mean if he spreads it around, he would miss out on the award trips and bonuses."

"Do you mind telling me which company it is?"

She seemed to hesitate. "Well, I guess it's no secret. Foster Insurance Company."

Josh made a mental note to check them out further with Roo. There was a note in Roo's file from Foster to close her investigation. "So he wrote Guinette Blakeley's policy with Foster?"

The blond straightened in her chair. "You'll have to ask Mr. Pratt about that. I'll slip him a note that you're waiting on him."

When she returned, she seemed less friendly, beauty

queen-ish and sterner gatekeeper-ish. "He'll be with you in a few minutes. He's finishing up now." She stared at the computer screen, sending a clear signal she was finished with Josh.

CHAPTER 28

Less than five minutes later, Pratt's office door opened and he walked his new customer to the front door. "Thanks again for your business. We appreciate it."

Pratt's smile diminished somewhat as he turned to Josh. "I understand you want to talk with me. Come on into my office." He turned to the blond. "Hold my calls." The full smile returned as he turned back to Josh. "I want to give our police chief my undivided attention."

Pratt's office was standard fare for most insurance offices: executive-size gray metal desk, cushioned desk chair on swivel rollers, and walls filled with awards and photos. Pratt was apparently active in numerous civic groups, in and near Blakeley, which wasn't unusual given his occupation. Several pictures caught Josh's eye: one was a photo of Pratt with Governor Larkin and another with Miller Blakeley. Again, nothing unusual about the photos. Most insurance agents networked constantly to drum up business. What did catch Josh's eye was the number of sales awards from Foster Insurance. "Wow, you must really sell a lot of insurance for Foster."

"I sell a lot of insurance, period."

"I guess it helps to be the only agent in town."

Pratt's jaw tightened. "I have customers all over the state." He shifted in his chair. "What can I do for you today? Is this personal or business?"

"I think I have all the life insurance I need. But I'd like to talk to you about Guinette Blakeley's policy."

"I thought I had answered all of that insurance investigator's questions."

"That investigation is between Ms. Murray, you, and the insurance carrier, of course. I'm here on a police matter. When you heard about Guinette's alleged suicide, what was your reaction?"

Josh studied Pratt's face but it was deadpan, revealing nothing.

"My reaction? Of course, I was sad for Miller. What a tragedy for him and his family."

"And for her, of course."

"Yes, of course. Especially since no one realized she was that depressed."

Josh detected a slight clinching in Pratt's jaw, which tightened his entire face. "One thing I'm curious about though. You've won all these awards from Foster Life Insurance. Is that why they agreed to waive the underwriting health exam on Guinette?"

Another slight clinching in Pratt's jaw. "Where are you going with all this?"

"I'm just saying that perhaps if she had been examined, her depression might have been discovered and treated."

Pratt sat up in his chair. "Now look here. Are you trying to blame me for her suicide?"

"Not at all. Just trying to understand why they would waive an exam on a policy of that size. I mean, maybe $5 million isn't much to you, but to me that's a pretty big policy. They didn't have kids, and surely he wasn't planning on giving her a $5 million funeral."

Pratt tugged at the collar of his shirt, as though it was irritating his neck. "It's not my place as an insurance agent to question why a husband buys a life insurance policy on his wife. You're trying to make all this sound unusual, but it's not." Pratt glanced at his phone, checking the time. "I have a potential client coming in soon. Do you have any more questions?"

"Just one more." Josh gestured toward the photos on the wall. "You and Miller Blakeley seem to be close friends. I see several photos of you two together."

Pratt tugged at his collar again. "We golf together and we're in a number of clubs together. Kiwanis, Lions Club, that kind of thing in various places near here."

"Is there any reason Miller would want his wife dead, other than for this big insurance payoff?"

Pratt stood up. "As far as I know, they had a good marriage. Now I really do need to run some numbers for this next meeting. If you have further questions, just call for an appointment. We stay pretty busy here."

When Josh got back to the police station, he asked Officer Holden to search Pet's farm for anything related to Abigail Sullivan.

CHAPTER 29

When Officer Holden arrived at Pet's farm, he saw an elderly man in a field beside the house. He was hand-feeding a small goat. "How you doing, Sir? I'm with the Blakeley PD, you got a minute?"

The man walked toward Holden. "How can I help you?"

"You're the caretaker here, right?"

"Yep, me, I'm Will, and my wife Nellie, we take care of the place. Or try to anyway."

"I'm looking for boxes that Abigail Sullivan may have left here. Do you know anything about that?"

"Yep, she did. Got some up there in the house. She came about three times to drop things off. Pet told her it was okay. She's a bit of a pack rat, Pet I mean, and she doesn't stay here all the time, so the place is a bit untidy right now. We don't do much on the inside. We mostly take care of the few goats here, some chickens, and the land."

"Mind if I have a look inside?"

"Not at all. Come on in, and I'll show you the boxes I know of. Can't say for sure this is all of them. I think Nellie might have put some in the attic, but I'm not sure. She's gone to the market where we sell eggs, or I'd ask her. None of the boxes are labeled, but you're welcome to look through 'em. Me and Nellie don't go snooping around in the house. Not our job."

Officer Holden smiled. "I get it." He followed Will into

the farmhouse. It looked to be at least fifty years old and had white siding and faded Charleston green shutters.

"There are some boxes in here. It's the bedroom Pet uses mostly to store stuff. Poor Abigail. Her falling down those stairs was a real tragedy. And that kid Timmy. He loves coming here. Asked Pet one time if he could stay with us." Will smiled. "Thank goodness, she said no. Minding kids is a young person's game, know what I mean?"

"Got two little ones myself, so I definitely get it. I'll just start looking around."

"I'll leave you be then," Will said as he walked out of the room.

Over the next hour, Holden went through every box in the room. As Will warned, none of them were labeled, so he had no idea who the contents belonged to. But Josh told him to look for journals and documents, so he did. After several hours of searching, he found neither.

Holden found the disappearing stairs to the attic Will mentioned and pulled down the steps. At the top, he reached for the light, a bare bulb with a chain pull. The place was dusty and downright spooky, and he was tired. Holden did a half-hearted search of a couple of boxes nearest the stairs before giving up.

CHAPTER 30

When Josh returned home that evening, Timmy was watching *Ghostbusters* on Enid's iPad. "That's an old one," Josh said.

"Timmy doesn't know that. He's been laughing since he began watching it. That's a good sign."

"Did Roo get settled next door? I left her a message that it was okay for her to stay there."

"Yes, she texted me earlier."

"I need to talk to her. I'm going to grab a quick bite of whatever that is that smells so good and then head over there."

"Are you making any progress on your investigation?"

Josh shrugged. "Not sure." He cut the chicken breast on the plate Enid had set in front of him. "You and Timmy already eaten?"

Enid nodded. "Sorry, he was hungry."

"That's good. I mean good that he has an appetite."

"I invited Roo to join us but she had a report she needed to do."

Josh finished off the chicken breast in a few bites. "Sorry to eat and run but I want to talk to Roo before she gets ready for bed."

Enid kissed him. "Go on. I'm used to being a police widow."

Josh texted Roo to let her know he was coming over. "I'll

take her one of those pastries she likes so much if you have any left."

"I saved one for you, but I know she'd like to have it." Enid wrapped the blueberry sweet roll in aluminum foil. "Tell her I said hello."

. . .

Roo was downstairs at the thrift shop waiting to let Josh in. "I see you come bearing gifts. Roo took the foil packet from him. "Aw, you're such a good guy. I'd share, but I'm starving. Somehow I missed lunch again, and Enid invited me to dinner but I had some work to do."

"Mind if I ask you a few questions? I know it's been a long day for both of us." He held out a file. "Oh, and you accidentally left this file behind."

"Thanks. I'm always forgetting something," she said as she winked. "Did you find out anything today?"

"Tell me about Foster Life Insurance Company. Do you do a lot of work for them?"

"No, actually this is only my second case with them. I did an investigation years ago, but we butted heads and I hadn't heard from them in a while. And this one wasn't actually assigned to me initially. I'm filling in for one of their guys who had a motorcycle accident. They asked me to get the investigation going, assuming he'd be back at work to take it over later. But the accident was more serious than they thought. The clock was running on their sixty days, so they asked me to finish it up to satisfy the auditors."

"Sounds like they didn't want you to dig too deep."

"It's not that unusual for a company to do a quicker investigation for an insurance agent who makes them a ton of money. Not exactly aboveboard, but not illegal either."

"At least not as long as the policy is legit and the death isn't questionable."

Roo threw her hands in the air. "Exactly. I know they were upset that I questioned this payout."

"And they know that we now have an open police investigation?"

Roo laughed. "Yeah, and believe me, they're not too happy with you or me right now. Doubt I'll get any more cases from them."

"So other than cutting a few corners, you don't have any reason to suspect the company isn't legit?"

Roo shrugged. "I have no reason to question the company. Only their judgment, at least on Guinette's case. But then I only work with a few people in the claims department. I have no dealings with the sales part or the rest of the company." She paused. "What makes you question them?"

"Nothing in particular. It just seems they are really cozy with Andy Pratt. But, as you said, he's one of their top agents, so I guess that's understandable. I'm just checking off the boxes." Josh stood. "You alright staying here? I mean it was a crime scene."

"Thanks for reminding me. But I know the police chief is next door, so it's all good."

"Just one more question. Do you know any of the private investigators who work this area? And one that's connected enough to do work for the governor?"

"This is really good." Roo wiped cream cheese icing from

her mouth with the back of her hand. "I can think of one or two, but I can give it some more thought. Why are you asking?"

"The governor hired someone to check into Guinette's death, or at least to do a background check on Miller Blakeley, but the file only referenced an investigator. There were no names or initials in the file, and I need to talk to him . . . or her."

Roo threw her hands in the air, sending a spray of crumbs flying. "Sorry. But when you said that, I just thought of someone who told me she had done some background work for a 'really high-up' guy in state government. I didn't pay much attention because I thought she was just bragging. Her name is Tiffany. I don't have her last name or contact info, but I know she has an office in downtown Columbia. She shouldn't be hard to find." She grinned. "If it's not her, I'll give you the names of a few others you can check out."

"By the way, what's the guy's name you report to at Foster? In case I need to talk to him."

"Nathan Adams. We call him Nate." She paused. "Funny thing, though. When I met with him the other day, someone higher up in the organization was the one who grilled me. Nate was there but didn't say a word. It was kinda weird."

CHAPTER 31

The next day, Josh made a few calls to his contacts and quickly found a female private investigator in Columbia named Tiffany. Her office was in The Vista, a trendy area near the Congaree River known for its restaurants and arts, along with a few businesses as well. It's designated as a South Carolina Cultural District to preserve its cultural, architectural, and historic heritage.

Tiffany's investigation company was located on the second floor of one of the older brick buildings just off Gervais Street. Josh didn't like elevators in general, and especially not the ones in old buildings that looked like freight elevators. So he took the stairs. Dozens of abstract art paintings lined the brick walls of the stairwell. He figured they must cost a lot because he didn't particular understand, or like, most of them.

Only a few offices were listed on the second-floor directory. Most of the other spaces were art galleries and studios. Tiffany's office was at the end of the hallway. Following the instructions on the small sign beside the door, Josh rang the doorbell. After no one appeared, he rang it again and waited. He had turned to leave when he heard the door open.

"May I help you?" The brunette who opened the door looked more like a model than a private investigator. However, Josh's contacts spoke highly of her, so he pushed his first impression aside.

"Are you Tiffany?"

She scanned Josh from head to toe, zeroing in on his name tag. "Yes, Chief Hart, I am. How can I help you?"

"May I come in? I'll be brief."

With a slight scowl on her face, she opened the door and motioned for Josh to come in. "This is a classy place," he said. "Not what I expected for a PI."

Tiffany laughed. "You've watched too many down-and-out gumshoe shows on TV. Some of us appreciate the finer things in life."

Josh looked around. "I can see that. And I apologize for stereotyping your profession."

"That's okay. I assume most police chiefs are fat and stupid. You're clearly not either." Tiffany motioned for Josh to sit on a small sofa in the reception area. The mid-century style frame was expensive looking wood, likely cherry, polished to a deep glow. The cushions were coarse ivory wool.

"Beautiful sofa."

"Thanks. My dad gave it to me when I opened the business. He was a private investigator also, not around here though. I went to USC and decided I liked it here. So I stayed." She flashed a beauty-queen smile, showing perfect teeth. Dad probably paid for that too. "But you're not here about my office decor. How can I help you?"

Josh leaned forward and rested his forearms on his legs. "First of all, I'm here in peace, so you can relax. I'm the police chief in Blakeley." He detected a slight switch in Tiffany. "I'm conducting an investigation of Guinette Blakeley's alleged suicide." He paused and then decided to jump in headfirst. "I believe you've also investigated that case."

Tiffany smoothed the leg of her black silk trousers and pinched the crease with her fingers. "If I had, I couldn't talk to you." She winked. "You know, client confidentiality and all that."

"I'll keep anything you give me confidential. I have no reason to expose you, but the clock is ticking, and if I don't prove my case soon, a murderer will get away with it and get paid a big sum of money. I know you did some work for Governor Larkin." He pointed to a photo on the wall. Larkin was in a tux and Tiffany was in a crimson red evening gown that clearly showed her assets.

"I paid for a table seat at that ball, like hundreds of other people. That's just a courtesy photo."

Josh laughed. "I thought you said I wasn't stupid. I know Larkin and if he took his photo with you, then he knows you pretty good. So let's stop being coy. Deal?"

"I like you. Too bad you've got that ring on your finger. You have kids?"

"Let's stick to my questions and I'll be out of here as quickly as I can. I saw your report in Larkin's private file on Miller Blakeley. You said in the report you thought Miller killed his wife. Just tell me why and how you came to that conclusion, and we can keep all this our little secret."

Tiffany waved her arm around the reception area. "I've got a good thing going here, and I'd like to keep it. And I'm not some stupid bimbo who does shoddy investigations just for big money." She pouted her lips. "Besides, the state doesn't pay as much as you'd think. I do work for large corporations also."

Josh held up both hands in surrender. "Whoa. I didn't mean to touch a nerve. In fact, when I was looking for you, everyone I talked to said you were one of the best. So let's just assume we're both good at what we do and help each other, confidentially of course."

"Sorry, it's just that—"

"You don't have to apologize. You're an attractive woman, and I'm sure you get your fair share of resentment from other women and too much attention from men. Now what can you tell me about Miller Blakeley?"

"To put it bluntly, he is a first-class asshole, a drug user, and a pusher."

Josh laughed. "Well, that's pretty clear. But none of that makes him a murderer."

"It does if his wife felt that way too and was about to turn him in."

Josh sat up straight. "Wait, you mean Guinette was going to turn Miller in for drug trafficking?"

"According to my source, yes. She knew it was only a matter of time before he was caught and with that landing strip practically in her back yard, it was hard for her to turn a blind eye to all of his trips to Mexico and the late-night visitors."

"Did she have proof that he was dealing?"

"You know he stole money from her, right?"

Josh nodded.

"When she confronted him, he threatened to kill her."

"How do you know this?"

"Abigail Sullivan told me. She overheard the conversation."

Josh leaned back on the sofa and ran his hands through his hair. "Wait, you talked to Abigail Sullivan before she died and she told you Guinette was going to turn him in? Are you sure?"

Tiffany laughed. "Of course I'm sure."

Josh exhaled a deep breath. "That means Larkin suspected Miller of his wife's death from the get-go. Why didn't you tell the authorities? You might have saved Abigail's life."

"If you're asking me why I didn't pull out my crystal ball, the one where I saw Miller push her down the stairs, then, gee, why didn't I think of that?" She leaned forward. "I gave my information to Larkin, my client, who assured me he would handle the information appropriately. Don't you think I've lost sleep thinking about the way things turned out?"

Josh held up his hands in surrender. "Sorry. It's just that this is such a huge revelation. Of course, you had no way of knowing what would happen."

"And none of this proves Miller actually killed Abigail."

"Why did she tell you all this?"

"I'm guessing it was a form of protection, or at least she thought it was. She must have sensed things were not going well."

"But you said Abigail felt Guinette was in danger."

Tiffany's eyes scanned the row of photos on the wall, including the one that featured her and the governor. "Even if I had wanted to, I had nothing concrete I could go to the authorities with. Not to mention, my client was the top law enforcement official in the state. It wasn't my call to make." She paused. "Now it's your turn. What's your story?"

"When Enid, that's my wife, and I decided to leave Madden, I was approached by Larkin. He asked if I would take the police chief job in Blakeley as a cover to investigate possible gang involvement with drug trafficking in the area. It made sense because at one time I had been on a drug task force the governor created. He never mentioned Miller Blakeley directly."

"Not surprised."

"We were in Blakeley nearly a year before Guinette's death. The coroner ruled it a suicide and that was the extent of my knowledge. An open and shut case. Then an insurance investigator raised questions about Guinette's death and refused to sign off on the report to the insurance company."

Tiffany tossed her head back and laughed. "Ruby-Grace Murray, right? That's the investigator?"

Josh nodded. "You know her?"

"We met briefly, but I know her by reputation. She can come across as a bit flaky, but she's one smart gal. And if she smells a rat, she'll chase it down like a coon dog."

Josh smiled. "I detected a bit of a Southern twang just now. Before that, I wasn't sure if you're from around here."

"Atlanta, the deep South part, not the transplanted part. My daddy and his family did well in the cotton business back in the day." She paused. "By the way, is your wife Enid Blackwell, the former reporter?"

"Yep, one and the same."

"She's pretty sharp herself. And a looker, as I recall from seeing her photo in the *State* newspaper." She shuddered. "That guy, the one who stalked her. That was really scary. And you were—"

"I'd rather not relive that experience, if you don't mind. Let's get back to Abigail. Did you have doubts when she allegedly fell down the steps?"

"Of course I did. And I confronted Larkin who assured me he was looking into it." She pressed her palms to her thighs. "Look, it's not my job to chase down the bad guys. That's your job. I just file my report."

"But it's not easy to walk away, is it?"

Tiffany's smile faded. "No, it's not."

CHAPTER 32

When Josh got back to Blakeley, Enid was closing the shop and Timmy was sitting in one of the chairs downstairs. "Hey, buddy. What you reading now?"

"It's about time travel. Do you think we can go back in time?"

Josh sat in the chair next to Timmy. "Well, I'm not sure. What do you think?"

Timmy's face scrunched a bit. "I don't think so. But I wish I could."

Josh wanted to get into comfortable clothes and shower off the day, but he knew this kind of thing was part of parenting, even if he was only temporarily in the role. "What would you do if you could?"

Again Timmy appeared to be thinking. "I would've got Nana to move from here. Maybe she'd still be . . ." His soft voice trailed off.

Josh tousled Timmy's hair. "I know, buddy. But there's nothing you could have done. Let's go upstairs and get something to eat."

"Miss Enid said we're having fish sticks."

Josh had never known Enid to eat processed fish. "Oh, that sounds good."

Timmy nodded. "I asked her if we could have them one day. Nana used to make them for me. I like lots of ketchup."

"Sounds . . . interesting. You stay here while I take a

shower. I'll come get you when dinner is ready."

Timmy had already shifted his focus back to the book.

. . .

Enid was making potato salad when Josh came into the kitchen. "Well, don't you look domestic," Josh said as he hugged her from behind. "And Timmy says we're having fish sticks."

Enid pointed to two tilapia fillets on the counter. "Timmy is, but we're having adult food."

Josh pulled her close to him again. "You never cease to amaze me. In fact, I was thinking how naturally you've taken to his whole motherhood thing."

Enid pulled away and turned to face him. "You can stop right there, mister. I'm doing the best I can, but don't get any ideas." She smiled. "I admit, Timmy is a sweetheart. I sure hope Pet pulls through and can take him again. He needs a real home, not an apartment over a shop."

Josh still longed for a shower, but the look on Enid's face concerned him. "Is that how you feel about living here? That it's not a real home?"

"It's home for us, but for a small child, I'm not sure. We can talk about this later. You take a shower and I'll sear these fillets."

. . .

After the kitchen was cleaned and the dishes put away, Josh took Enid's hand and led her to the sofa. "Let's talk a bit."

He smiled. "Timmy must have enjoyed the fish sticks. He gobbled them down, along with a half bottle of ketchup."

"Want me to make you some too next time?"

Josh shook his head. "No thanks, the tilapia was delicious. Your cooking has come a long way since I first met you." He put his arm around her and pulled her close. "You're amazing."

Enid rested her head on his shoulder. "What's on your mind? If you need to talk, I can listen."

Josh sighed. "I don't deserve you, but I'm glad you overlooked that fact and married me anyway." He buried his face in her hair and inhaled the faint scent of something floral. "Are you happy here? I mean running the shop, living in Blakeley?"

Enid shrugged. "Mostly. I mean it's pretty quiet around here. No stress or deadlines."

"But you miss reporting, don't you?"

"Sometimes." Enid sat up and turned to look at Josh. "What about you? Are you happy being a really-small-town police chief?" She then added, "Although I realize that's not all you're really doing."

"Well, yes, and no. I long for more complex policing at times. And I wish we were more accepted here."

"If what you think about Miller Blakeley is true, then this place is a hotbed of crime."

Josh nodded. "Yep. And I met with a female PI today who also does work for Larkin. She's convinced Miller is guilty."

"Does she have proof?"

"No, it's mostly circumstantial and the opinions of a few

people she talked to. She turned everything over to Larkin to do a criminal investigation."

"Which is what you're doing?"

Josh didn't answer.

"If you want to talk, I'm not a reporter any longer. Or have you forgotten that?"

"Ouch. I didn't mean to hit a nerve. I'm just so used to us having a conflict of interest. I want to tell you what I know because I need your reporter's instincts to help me."

"Really? You're not just saying that?"

"You kidding me? You investigated and solved some crimes law enforcement couldn't. Of course I value your instincts. And sometimes we lawmen can get so close to a case we miss the obvious."

Enid's face lit up. "So tell me where you are with the case."

Josh covered his investigation to date with Enid as they sipped coffee. When he finished, she leaned her head back against the sofa. "What a mess. Do you really think Miller killed Guinette?"

"Spouses kill their mates all the time, so that wouldn't be so unusual, but killing Abigail, now that's a stretch for me. With Miller's reputation in town, if it came down to he-said-she-said, most people would believe Miller."

"The first thing I want to do is get Jack's files, if he has any, on Miller Blakeley or anything at all on the town of Blakeley. You know we can trust him."

Josh nodded as he sipped coffee.

"And then I want to talk to Timmy again."

"Whoa, now we're getting into dicey territory. If child

protective services ever gets wind of us interrogating a child, we've got trouble."

"I'm not going to *interrogate* him. We're taking care of him, for Pete's sake. It's natural curiosity for us to know who to protect him from."

"Okay, just tread lightly. And let me know what you find out. By the way, is he in bed? It's getting late."

"Abigail trained him well. He knows to brush his teeth and then he reads for a little while and turns out the light. He's nearly a perfect kid."

"Do I detect—?"

"No, stop it."

Josh laughed. "But seriously, after this is all over, we need to plan our future. Again. A life that includes what you want."

Enid kissed him on the nose. "You're sweet."

CHAPTER 33

Enid reflected on her conversation with Josh last night, and once again was grateful that Timmy was such a good kid. Otherwise, this whole experience could have been a disaster. After a breakfast of cereal and milk, he settled down to study. He would be signing onto his remote classes soon. Thankfully, he enjoyed learning, and his instructor made sure he stayed mentally challenged.

She straightened up the kitchen and went downstairs to call Jack since she had almost an hour before the shop opened. Today there was a small group of ladies coming in who wanted to form a book club, and they planned to begin meeting regularly at the shop. In return, they committed to buying their books from her instead of Amazon, as they typically did. Small bookstores can't offer everything the big guys do, but the online sellers can't offer a cozy bookstore, fresh coffee, and homemade snacks.

When Jack answered her call, he seemed surprised. "Well, well. Have you finally come to your senses and kicked that nearly perfect man of yours to the curb for a slightly older version?"

Enid laughed. "Is this a good time? I need to ask for your help again on something."

"Perfect time. Ginger is out tracking down whoever may have vandalized the old Pinewood cemetery, and I've finished my story on the town council. You'll be happy to know the historical society will continue to be funded. Of course, the historian position has been open for a couple of years now. But the right person will come along."

"Josh and I need to visit Madden again soon. Perhaps after this case is over. But right now I need to see if you have any information on Miller or Guinette Blakeley. And add Abigail Sullivan to the list. In fact, just anything you or Ginger can find on Blakeley or anyone in the town would be helpful.

"What exactly am I looking for? Anything specific? Or just anything related to Guinette's suicide, which I'm assuming hasn't been put to rest yet, or you wouldn't be calling me. Oh, and are you calling for you or for Josh? I'm just curious if you're reporting again."

"It's more for Josh, but I want to know too. I think he's hit a brick wall, and he's asked me to think about the case like a reporter. I know Blakeley isn't in your tri-county reporting area, but some of these things spill over the border, especially something as newsworthy as this whole mess."

"Will do. I'll get Ginger to help too. Research, as you know, is one of her many strengths. You'd be proud of how well she's developed."

"I'm glad, for both of you."

"Before you go, how's the woman that was abducted? I heard she was in the hospital."

"She's doing fair. With her history of heart problems, she's having a tough recovery."

"And what about the little guy staying with you?"

"Timmy is a good kid, and he's still here. I just hope things settle down for him soon. He deserves a better life than he's gotten."

"I know what you mean, but he's lucky to have you and Josh taking care of him in the meantime. Maybe you can bring him to visit the ranch one day. We've got several horses boarded here now. He might enjoy seeing them."

"He'd love that. He has a natural curiosity about everything, and I'd love for him to meet you. Oh, speaking of love, have you found the perfect mate yet?"

"Nah, I'm still a happy widower. I date now and then, and Madelyn and I stay in touch, but now that she's in the state legislature, she has little time for a small fry like me."

"Well, I'm glad you're happy, at least. Let me know if you find anything."

• • •

Enid waited until after lunch to talk to Timmy. "How did school go today?"

Timmy shrugged. "Okay."

"Nothing interesting in your lessons?"

Another shrug.

"I've got another new ghost book downstairs for you."

"Can I go read it now?"

"How about I make you some hot chocolate and we can talk for a few minutes first? Is that okay?"

"I did my lessons."

"This is not about school. I'd like to ask you a few questions about Abigail. Would you mind talking about her?"

"No, I guess it's okay."

Enid made Timmy a cup of instant hot chocolate and

brought it to him. "I put little marshmallows in it." Enid made a mental note to clean out all the kid food when Timmy went back to live with Pet. Even though he was a nearly perfect kid, taking care of him, worrying about his meals, and just plain worrying about him was a full-time job. She had always assumed parenting would be all consuming, but experiencing it was another thing altogether. She waited until Timmy had taken a few sips.

"I know you miss Abigail. You called her Nana, right?"

Timmy nodded as he licked the chocolate from his lips. "She made hot chocolate from scratch."

Enid laughed. "But that's something special only grand-mas do. How did she make it?"

Timmy explained how she put chocolate from a brown can and milk in a pot and stirred it. His face lit up when he added, "She even put chocolate chips in it. You know, like the ones in cookies."

"Well, one day you'll have to show me how to make it."

But Timmy just looked at her and she realized she had stepped over the line. "But that was something special for you and Nana." She paused, unsure how to proceed. "You've said a couple of times she wanted to leave Blakeley. Why was that?"

Timmy looked up and made direct eye contact with Enid. "She was scared." His young face suddenly seemed pale.

"What do you think she was afraid of?" She stopped when Timmy's eyes filled with tears. "I wouldn't ask if it wasn't important. I'd never want to upset you. But did she mention anyone's name or anything specific she was afraid of?"

Timmy was silent for a moment. "She said this was a bad town for bad people. She said they got away with bad things."

"Did you know what she was talking about?"

Timmy shook his head. "No, but she got real scared after Miss Ginny died and some man came to see her."

"Is that what you called Guinette Blakeley?"

A faint smile appeared on his face for the first time since they started talking. "I couldn't say her name when I was a little kid so they told me to call her Miss Ginny."

"Do you know who it was that came to see Nana?"

Timmy shook his head.

"Do you know what happened to Miss Ginny?"

"Nana said she went to heaven."

"That's right, she did. Did Nana say anything else about Miss Ginny?"

Timmy's face scrunched as it did when he was concentrating. Often when Enid would check on him while he was in his virtual classes, she would find him glued to the screen with that same intense look. "Nana said Miss Ginny didn't want to go to heaven. Not yet. And she told me not to believe what people said about her. She made me promise."

Enid took a deep breath, unsure how much further to push him. "Just one more question, okay?"

Timmy nodded.

"Did Nana tell you what suicide means?"

"She told me it's when you don't want to live anymore. She told me about some famous writer who wanted to die."

"You mean Ernest Hemingway, the writer?"

Timmy smiled. "Yeah, that's him. She said Miss Ginny's

husband liked him."

"Yes, sadly, Hemingway was a great writer, and considering Blakeley's history, I'm not surprised that's the example she gave you."

"I read about him, but Nana said I wasn't old enough to read his stories."

"Probably true. But why did Nana say Miss Ginny didn't want to die?"

Timmy shook his head. "I don't know, but after that Nana got real scared." He put the empty mug on the table. "I like your hot chocolate too." He wrapped his small arms around Enid's neck and held onto her.

"Thank you. I'm glad you like it." Enid's cell phone rang and she saw Josh's face on the screen. "Hey. I'm just sitting here with Timmy. We're having our little talk."

"Pet is back in ICU. She's had a heart attack."

CHAPTER 34

It was nearly 3:00 a.m. when Josh got home. Enid woke up when he came into the bedroom and could tell from his face the news wasn't good. "How is Pet doing?" she asked, sitting up in bed.

"She's hanging on but the doctor doesn't think she'll make it much longer. Her heart was already weak before all this happened. The nurse delivered a message to me that Pet gave her not long before her heart attack." He paused. "She wanted me to promise we'd find a good home for Timmy. She said Abigail had put the names of some distant relatives in one of her journals. But of course, we don't have those."

"We've got to find them. For several reasons."

"When I visited Pet earlier, she gave me permission to search her farm for anything related to Abigail or Guinette. But Officer Holden said he couldn't find anything. The caretaker who maintains the place said he remembered Abigail visiting the farm several times to leave boxes, but they weren't labeled. Holden said there were lots of boxes and he had no idea which might have been Abigail's. But he couldn't find any with documents or journals."

"Poor Timmy. He's been through so much. I'll start looking at Abigail's ancestry online. Maybe I can turn up some relatives. Oh, and I talked to Jack. He's going to see what he can find, and he said to tell you hello."

Josh sat on the bed beside Enid and pulled her close. "I

know you miss Jack and the life you had in Madden. I promise when all this is over, we'll go wherever you want to—
back to Madden or someplace new."

"We can worry about all that later. You seem to think I'm
so unhappy, but I'm not." She smiled and held up her index
finger and thumb with an inch gap between them. "Okay,
maybe I'm feeling about this much unfulfilled. It's odd not
having deadlines. Maybe I need to focus more on marketing
the bookstore, you know, holding some signings or events
here."

Josh kissed her. "We'll figure it out."

A scream suddenly came from down the hall. Enid flung
back the covers and ran to Timmy's room. He was sitting
up in bed, tears streaming from his face. "Nana told me to
be brave, but I'm scared. Are you going to take me to an
orphan home?"

Enid hugged Timmy. "No, I promise we'll never do
that." She turned to look at Josh. "Will we?"

Josh sat beside Enid. "No, buddy. We won't."

Enid pushed Timmy's sandy hair back from his eyes.
"Did Nana come to see you again tonight?"

Timmy nodded.

"Did she tell you anything else?"

He looked into Enid's eyes. "She said you were a good
person and I should listen to you."

"The next time you talk to Nana, you tell her I said,
'thank you.' Now let's get you back to bed." Enid helped
Timmy get back under the covers.

"That man had a suit on."

"What man is that?"

"The one Nana was afraid of."

Enid glanced at Josh. "Did you see him?"

"I don't know. Maybe."

"We'll talk about it in the morning. Goodnight." Enid kissed Timmy's forehead, trying not to let her worry show.

• • •

The next morning, just as Josh was getting ready to leave for the station, he got a phone call from the hospital. "Thanks for letting me know. I'll have someone contact you about arrangements."

Enid poured herself another cup of tea. "Pet died, didn't she?"

Josh nodded. "Not unexpected but still sad." He pointed to her cup. "You're back on tea again?"

Enid smiled. "I missed my Earl Grey." She took a sip. "Who will handle the arrangements? Does she have relatives?"

"I don't know, but I'm going out to her farm to talk to the two caretakers, Will and Nellie. Maybe they know who to contact." He pointed upstairs. "Do you want me to tell Timmy?"

"I can do that. You go ahead. Maybe you can talk with him later tonight when you get home."

CHAPTER 35

When Josh arrived at Pet's farm, it was as if Will and Nellie were expecting him. The news of Pet's death didn't seem to surprise them. "She was a good ol' gal," Will said. "But her heart was plum wore out." He crossed himself, which surprised Josh, as there weren't many Catholics in this area. Out in rural areas like this, Southern Baptists seemed to be the most prevalent religion, with a few Methodists and Lutherans thrown in. "May she rest in peace," Will added.

"We've been expecting you or someone to come tell us Pet was gone." Nellie wiped her eyes with an old-fashioned white handkerchief with a lacy border. "What will happen to Timothy?"

"Well, that's why I'm here."

"We're too old to take on a small child. Besides, we aren't kin," Will said. "He's a good boy, but parenting is for younger folks. That's what I told your officer." He looked up toward the sky. "Poor boy's had a rough young life. Don't seem fair sometimes. Know what I mean?"

Josh nodded. "Do you know any of Pet's relatives, cousins or anyone?"

"I've got all her paperwork in a folder," Nellie said. "When we found out she had a heart attack, I started pulling all her papers together. Not much to go on." She sighed and looked at Will. "Guess we'll have to find another place to live." She looked back at Josh. "There's a will too. Or so it says on one of the envelopes. Didn't open it. Figured it was none of my business. I'll get it all for you."

Josh wanted to give them some assurances, but he had no idea what plans Pet might have made or who would inherit the farm. "Thanks. I need to make arrangements with the hospital. Did you see anything in her papers about her funeral wishes?"

"Didn't look. I'll go get the files now."

Josh sat with Will while Nellie went to the back of the house. "How long you been working here?"

Will smiled. "Never think of it as working. This has been our home for near to forty years. We live in a cabin on the edge of the farm. Can't see it from here. We began working for Pet's parents, then when she inherited the farm, she asked us to stay." He paused and rubbed his forehead. "Funny, but you're the second person to ask that."

"What do you mean?"

"Some guy came here not long ago. Wanted to look around in case he wanted to buy the place. Told him it weren't for sale. He asked how long we'd worked here. Told him the same thing—near to forty years."

"Do you get people wanting to buy this place often? I mean, no offense, but it's pretty remote."

"He was the first one I can remember. It's a good little farm, been passed down through Pet's family. We get a little income from raising and selling pygmy goats, and Nellie takes the eggs to the little store down the road. But Pet never tried to make any money on this place. Reason she kept it, she said, was because she had an idea she'd sell the shop one day and retire here. 'Course she retired once already. I think she got bored, the reason she opened the shop."

Nellie walked into the room with an armload of papers. "Guess it was more than I remembered. I got a cardboard box in the kitchen I can put it all in if you want."

"That'd be great, thanks," Josh said.

"I heard Will telling you about the man who stopped by here not long ago. He wouldn't tell us much about himself. Only that he heard about this property from a friend. Me and Will figured he was buying it for a dude ranch or something. What else would a guy in a suit like that want to do out here?"

Josh felt a chill grip him. "A suit?" *That man had a suit on.*

Will nodded. "Looked like one of them Brooks Brothers suits all the banker folks used to wear. I only had one or two suits in my life. Both came from Sears and Roebuck Company. Good suits, they were."

"Did he tell you his name?" Josh asked.

Will and Nellie exchanged glances and then both shook their heads. "Not that I recall," Will said. "In fact, I remember asking him but he never said. I asked him if he had a card, but he didn't. Anybody wearing a suit like that has a card. When we wouldn't let him look around, he just left."

"Was this before or after Pet was abducted?"

"Right before, as I recall." He looked at Nellie, who nodded in agreement.

Josh pulled a card from his pocket and smiled. "I don't have but one suit, and it's for weddings and funerals. But I got a card. Call this number if you see that man again or remember anything, no matter how small, that might help with Pet's arrangements. I'll go through this paperwork today."

. . .

Timmy took the news of Pet's death stoically, without tears or visible emotion, which concerned Enid. He had lost his parents, his grandmother, and now the person his Nana had asked to care for him. Enid wanted to cry, not just for Pet but for Timmy. But she kept her composure.

"I know you're worried about where you will go. For now, you'll stay right here." Trying to think of something hopeful to say, she added. "My friend Jack has a horse ranch. He wants you to come see him. Would you like that?"

Timmy looked up into her eyes. "For just a visit? Or will I have to stay there?"

Enid grabbed Timmy and held him close. "Just for a visit. And I'll be with you. You can ride the horses, or just pet them. Jack would love to meet you."

Timmy's head rubbed against her chest as he nodded. "Okay." He pulled away. "I want to stay with you."

Enid gave up holding back the tears. "I know but . . ." She had no words to finish the sentence. "Let's just take it one day at a time. We won't make you go anywhere you don't want to. I promise." She hoped Josh wouldn't feel compelled to call child welfare to report Timmy was an orphan. And she prayed they would find a suitable relative soon. She might need more of a purpose in life, but being an instant mother wasn't what she had in mind, no matter how great a kid Timmy was. "I'll let your teachers know what happened, so you won't have to go to classes for a few days."

"I want to go. Please."

Enid smiled. "Of course you can. I'm glad you like school so much."

Timmy went back to his room, and Enid decided he might need some time alone, so she didn't try to dissuade him. She tapped on Roo's phone number to send a text. "Pet died."

CHAPTER 36

Josh came home early in the afternoon, carrying a cardboard box. "I got these papers from Pet's farm. I'm going upstairs to go through them. Maybe we can find something helpful." He started up the stairs. "How's Timmy?"

"He's putting on a brave front, but he's scared he'll have to go to an orphanage."

Josh kissed Enid on the cheek. "We've got to make sure that doesn't happen."

Upstairs, he laid out the papers on the dining table. Some were copies of paid bills, so he put those in a stack. As he went through organizing the contents, he found the envelope Will had mentioned. Some lawyer had told him once not to mess with anything relating to a will, so Josh reluctantly put the envelope aside. He'd have to get some legal advice on what to do with it.

After an hour, Josh still had not found anything that gave him a clue on how to proceed with Pet's funeral arrangements. He looked through his contacts and tapped on a number.

When Tiffany answered, her smooth voice oozed, "Well, well. If it's not my handsome police chief. How can I help you?"

"I need an attorney, one that specializes in estates. Can you recommend one?"

The shift in Tiffany's voice was unmistakable—all

business. "Sure. Got a pen? I'll give you the contact information."

Josh wrote down the name and phone number. "Can I tell him you referred me?"

Tiffany laughed. "Morgan is a woman. She was my college roommate. And, yes, please tell her I said hello."

"Thanks, I owe you one."

"You bet you do. But call me anytime."

He tapped Morgan's number into his phone. The woman who answered explained Morgan was busy, but when he mentioned Tiffany's name, the woman asked him to hold.

In less than a minute, another woman greeted him. "What in the hell are you doing messing around with Tiffany?" She laughed. "She's nothing but trouble. And you tell her I said that. Anyway, what do you need?"

Josh explained Pet's death and the envelope he found. "Well, I appreciate your taking caution. It's okay to open it but don't remove any staples from the will or do anything that might make it look altered. Just to be cautious though, I'm going to put you on Zoom and record your opening the envelope. Are you good with that? And you do have Zoom on your phone, right?"

Josh laughed. "Even us small-town cops have *some* tech savvy."

"Good. Now I'll send you a link and you can end this call and get on Zoom. I'll set up the meeting and then let you open it. And I'll need a fee from your office."

Josh's heart sank. "How much will that be? We're a small police department."

Morgan's raucous laugh again. "How about a dollar? Can

you swing that? And you can donate it to charity."

Josh exhaled deeply. "I think we can manage that."

When they connected on Zoom, Morgan introduced herself and then said. "I am with Police Chief Josh Hart. His department has retained me for legal advice on the estate of a deceased crime victim. He has been given personal papers of the deceased and he will open the envelope labeled 'Last Will and Testament' so that his department can notify the administrator or whoever is identified in the will. Have I stated the situation correctly, Chief Hart?"

"You have."

"Since I am recording this meeting, please make sure you open the envelope so that it's visible to the camera. You may proceed."

Josh had logged onto the Zoom call with his laptop, so he held the envelope in front of the camera and opened it. Inside was a document that he held up to the camera.

"Please show me how many pages there are. I'd like to record each one on this call."

Josh went through each of the pages so that each was visible on camera. "That's all of it."

"Thank you. Do not alter the pages in any way. Once you've found the named executor, give it to them in the original envelope. If there are any questions, you can refer them to me. I am now ending this recording."

Josh stayed on the call until the red recording button had disappeared. "Thanks for your help. If I need anything further, I'll find some funds to pay you."

"Tell Tiffany to pay me. She owes me for a lot of beers from our college days." She paused. "Tiffany is good people though. Don't let that act of hers make you think otherwise. Take care, Chief Hart."

CHAPTER 37

Pet's will did not appear to have been updated since it was originally signed nearly ten years ago. There were no amendments or other attachments. The farm had been left to Will and Nellie, and they were also her co-executors. She made the request that the farm not be sold to any developer. Josh knew, however, it was just a request. Nothing could legally stop Will and Nellie from selling the farm if they wanted to once the deed was transferred. And considering their ages, it was unlikely they wanted to take on the tax burden, maintenance, and all that comes with land ownership.

The thrift shop was leased but the contents were to be liquidated and the proceeds given to Will and Nellie for farm maintenance. Josh's heart stopped when he read the next line. All of Pet's personal belongings, which included all the family mementos, were to go to a cousin, Meredith, who lived in Oconee County.

Josh pushed the will aside and began an online search for Meredith. After thirty minutes, he found a likely candidate, although she looked a good bit younger than Pet. This woman was unmarried, according to her social media page, a retired schoolteacher, and lived in Oconee County in upstate South Carolina. Her Facebook page was filled with photos of mountain flora, streams and rivers, and photos of Meredith with friends.

He looked online on several search sites but couldn't find

a phone number. Josh texted the information to his officer Sam Holden, who was much more tech savvy than Josh and asked him to find Meredith's number.

While waiting for Sam's reply, Josh studied the photos, trying to discern any resemblance to Pet, but he saw none. And Meredith didn't mention any cousins or other relatives in her posts.

A chime signaled an incoming text from Sam, who sent Josh a possible phone number. When Josh called it, there was no answer. Maybe she didn't answer calls from unknown numbers, which was all too common these days due to the bombardment of spam calls. He left a message for Meredith to call immediately.

Josh picked up the will again and reread it, hoping to find other clues to Pet's family. When Josh's phone rang, he answered immediately. "Hello, this is Chief Hart."

The silence made Josh wonder if he, too, was a victim of a spam call, but he recognized the number he had just called. "Hello?" a female voice said.

"Yes, I'm here. Are you Meredith?" Josh asked.

Another brief silence. "I'm only returning your call because you said you were a police chief. Is this a prank call?"

Josh was glad Meredith couldn't see his smile. "No, ma'am, it's not. I am police chief in Blakeley, South Carolina." Before he could say anything further, he heard Meredith gasp.

"It's Pet, isn't it. Is she in trouble?"

"Are you related to her?" Josh asked. "I need to confirm who you are before I discuss anything with you."

"Okay, then." Meredith paused. "Petula, or Pet, as we

call her, runs a thrift shop and lives in Blakeley." Another pause. "I'm sorry but I don't know much else about her. You see, I haven't talked to her in years. We just lost touch, and I don't know why because there aren't many people left in our family."

Josh heard Meredith blow her nose.

"I'm sorry, it's just that . . . What else do you need to know before you can tell me what this is all about?"

"I'm sorry to inform you but your cousin has passed. She had a heart attack after sustaining injuries. I'm sorry for your loss."

The silence was so long, Josh thought they had been cut off. "Are you still there?"

"Yes. What kind of injuries?"

"I'd rather not talk about that on the phone. Do you live in Oconee County?"

"Yes, upstate near the Blue Ridge Mountains.

"Would it be possible for you to come down here and make burial arrangements?"

"Now?"

"As soon as possible. Unless you know someone else I should call. Right now, she's in a hospital morgue, waiting to be claimed."

"I didn't know Blakeley had a hospital."

"It doesn't, but I can send you directions to the hospital just down the highway."

"Blakeley was always a weird place, as far as I'm concerned. But Pet loved it. Wait, have you told Abigail? I can't remember her last name, but they were really close friends."

"Abigail Sullivan?" Josh said.

"Yes. Then you've talked to her."

"No, ma'am. I'll explain when you get here." Josh gave Meredith directions and told her there was a Hampton Inn nearby where she could stay.

"Alright. I'll be there late tonight. I have to find a pet sitter and wrap up a few things here."

"This is my cell number you called, so let me know when you're here, no matter what time." After ending the call, Josh heard Enid and Timmy talking in the guest room and wondered how he could keep his promise to both of them that Timmy wouldn't go to a foster home.

CHAPTER 38

At breakfast the next morning, Josh asked Timmy if he wanted to meet Pet's cousin. She had called about ten o'clock last night to confirm she had checked in and would meet him at the hospital morgue in the morning. Josh put his hand on Timmy's arm as reassurance. "She seems like a nice lady."

"Why?"

Josh glanced at Enid, who was giving him that "be careful" look. "Well, I just thought since she's related to Pet, you might want—"

"But she's not my family." Timmy looked at Josh, his brown eyes filled with tears.

Enid came over and put her arms around Timmy. "Maybe we can meet her together, sometime later when you're ready. Do you want to help me run the shop today?"

"I have to go to school."

"No, you don't. It's Saturday."

Timmy shrugged. "Does that mean Tess won't be bringing any cookies today?"

Enid tapped Timmy's nose gently. "I tell you what. She's bringing over snacks for a book club meeting, but I'll ask her to bring some of those chocolate brownies with nuts you like so much. Would you like that?"

Timmy's smile lit up his face, as he nodded.

"I need to talk to Josh for a few minutes. Can you go

down and wait for me there?"

Timmy jumped from his chair and headed down the stairs.

"You're so good with him."

"Please don't start. I just didn't want you to rush him into meeting Pet's cousin. Timmy's right. She's not related to him. What were you thinking?"

Josh ran his hand through his hair. "I guess I'm just desperately trying to find a solution to this whole thing with Timmy. But you're absolutely right, as usual."

"There's no reason to think Meredith would have a reason to take Timmy. You said her social media profile shows she's not married."

"Maybe her husband died. Or left. Maybe she has children."

"You go to the hospital and meet with Meredith. Timmy and I will eat brownies." She then added, "It seems pretty obvious all of this is connected."

"What? You mean Guinette, Abigail and Pet?"

Enid nodded.

"Maybe it's time for me to turn this mess over to SLED."

"But if you look at it on the surface, you have nothing to suggest Guinette didn't commit suicide. And we don't have any proof that Abigail's fall wasn't accidental. So that leaves Pet. We know she was abducted, but you can't prove there's a definite connection. I doubt any of this is enough to get a prosecutor excited. You need more proof."

"There you go, being right again." He kissed Enid's forehead. "Got to run."

• • •

In less than thirty minutes, Josh was sitting in the lobby of the Hampton Inn waiting for Meredith to come down. He thought he might recognize her from her online photos, but when she walked up to him, she looked even younger than he expected.

"Chief Hart?"

"Yes. Are you Meredith?"

She nodded.

"No offense, but you look much younger than those photos on your Facebook page."

"I don't know of any woman who would be offended by someone telling her she looks younger. I've just always had this young face, which is nice, I guess."

"But you're Pet's cousin?"

"She was actually my mother's cousin, which makes her my first cousin once removed."

"Is your mother still alive?"

Meredith shook her head. "Sadly, she died about twenty years ago. Heart attack. Sounds like it runs in the family." She glanced at the big clock in the lobby. "I guess we'd better go. But first, you said Pet had injuries. What was that all about?"

Josh motioned toward the door. "Let's get going, and I'll tell you on the way.

• • •

By the time Josh and Meredith got to the hospital lobby, he had filled her in on Pet's abduction and Abigail's fatal fall. "And there's more, I'm afraid."

"Oh my. Can it get any worse?"

"Did you ever meet Abigail's grandson Timmy?"

"No, I haven't. Why?"

Josh thought about Enid's warning last night. "I realize you're not related to Timmy, but he was living with Pet. Abigail asked her to take him in if anything happened to her."

Meredith frowned. "You mean Pet adopted him?"

"I don't think it was formalized, just an agreement, an arrangement."

A doctor approached Josh and Meredith. "Hello again, Chief Hart." He looked at Meredith. "And you must be the cousin."

"Once removed," she said.

"I'm sorry for your loss," the doctor said. "Come to the administration office with me, and they can walk you through the process. I need to get back upstairs on rounds." He turned to Meredith. "The state will likely want an autopsy in a case like this where a crime was committed. We've contacted them and will transfer the deceased to the coroner's office today. Even though Pet had a weak heart, her heart failure was likely brought on by the physical attack she endured."

Meredith nodded. "I understand."

CHAPTER 39

Enid and Timmy were enjoying brownies when her cell phone rang and she saw Jack's face on the screen. "Hey, Jack. Hold on a minute." She turned to Timmy. "I need to take this. Can you watch the shop? I'll be right upstairs."

Timmy looked around the empty shop and nodded. "Can I eat another brownie?"

"Sure. But just one. We don't want you to get fat." Enid turned her attention to Jack. "Hi, do you have something for me?"

Jack laughed. "Hello. Good to hear your voice. You sound a bit frazzled."

"A few things have happened since we talked. Pet, the thrift shop owner, died, and the young boy who lived with her is now with us."

"Wow. How are you and Josh handling all this?"

"We're okay, but all this domestic stuff is beginning to wear me down. I never thought I'd say this, but I miss writing obituaries."

"I sure wish I could record that comment to play back to you later when you deny it. If it makes you feel any better, Ginger hates writing them too. Are you trying to find a home for the boy?"

"No. I'm going to do an ancestry search on Abigail when I get a chance. It's been crazy around here." She filled him in on Meredith.

"Well, at least the body has been claimed. Wouldn't that be awful to be stuck in a hole somewhere with no family around to care."

"Josh and I would never have let that happen."

"I know. Anyway, here's what Ginger and I found out. By the way, before I start, I would really like for you to report on this for the *Tri-County Gazette* once it's all settled."

"Jack, you know I can't do that. Because of Josh. How would it look if the police chief's wife wrote about a case he was handling." She paused. "You must think there's some big news. Tell me what you found out."

"Maybe you can help Ginger with the story, as a confidential informant. But anyway, enough of holding you in suspense."

"Yes, please," Enid said.

"Well, it seems there was a quiet SLED investigation about drug trafficking in Blakeley."

"Quiet? What does that mean? And when was this?"

"Quiet just means unofficial, you know, off the books. It was about two years ago. Apparently, it was kept off the books. My SLED contact said they were told by someone high up on the food chain that no one was to talk about it or report on it."

"They can't do that. The public has a right to know."

Jack laughed. "You haven't been out of the business that long that you've forgotten how it works. No, they can't stop us from reporting, but they can go silent and then we're dead without insiders talking to us."

Enid sighed. "No, I haven't forgotten. Go on."

"So my contact said they suspected a prominent

businessman in Blakeley as being the ringleader of a white-collar drug enterprise."

"Miller Blakeley?" Enid asked.

"No. Andy Pratt."

Enid felt the air being sucked from her lungs. "The insurance agent?"

"One and the same. And get this. He had, or was suspected of having, an accomplice."

"Was it Miller Blakeley?"

"My contact wouldn't say."

"Jack, that's like tearing out the last page of a whodunit before you give it to someone to read. Why wouldn't he tell you?"

"He just said it may have involved someone out of state. They didn't have enough proof to arrest anyone or even open an official investigation. Or so they said."

Enid walked a little way down the stairs and sat on one of the steps so she could see Timmy, who was sitting in one of the chairs reading. "I need to tell Josh all this. He won't use your name, but this is enough for him to start digging on his own."

"I'll let you know if we find anything else. But tell Josh to be careful. This is no amateur drug ring. They've got money and connections."

• • •

By the time Enid composed herself and went downstairs, two of the book club members had arrived and were talking to Timmy. He was showing them around the shop. Enid realized she had not set out the folding chairs from the storage closet.

"Ladies, I'm so sorry. I had an urgent phone call I needed to take."

One of the ladies extended her hand. "I'm Emily and this is Joan. Your assistant has been giving us the tour."

"We're honored to have you meet here. Let me get those chairs out."

Timmy followed her. "I'll help."

Enid smiled. "You really are a great assistant. I think we need six chairs."

"That's right," Emily said. "The others are on the way."

After the chairs were put in a semicircle, Joan asked Enid, "I didn't know you had a child. You probably don't remember me, but we met when you first opened the shop."

"I'm sorry, I didn't recognize you. And Timmy is just staying with us for a while."

The shop door opened and four other women walked in. They all introduced themselves to Enid. After she had served coffee and passed around a tray of Tess's sweets, Enid excused herself. "Just call out if you need me. I'll be upstairs." She reached out for Timmy's hand. "Come on up with me so they can meet."

When they were upstairs, Enid hugged Timmy. "I'm so proud of you. You're growing up right in front of me. And you make a great book club host."

"Can I sit at the top of the stairs and watch?"

Enid knew the book they were discussing was safe enough for Timmy's ears. "Alright, but be really quiet, okay?"

"Yes, ma'am."

"I'm going to make a few phone calls. Let me know if they need anything."

Timmy nodded and smiled.

Enid made a mental note to give Timmy something he could be responsible for since it seemed to make him happy to be needed. She went into the bedroom but left the door open so she could hear Timmy if he called.

She tapped on Josh's cell number but got his voice mail. "I need to talk to you. Call me when you get this." Feeling guilty about abandoning both the book club and Timmy, she went to check on them. She sat next to Timmy on the top step.

One of the ladies was talking softly. "He's Abigail's grandson. Andy knew her."

Was she Andy Pratt's wife? Enid grabbed Timmy's hand. "Let go see what we can find for you to read. I've got a few books up here."

"That lady knew Nana?"

"It's a small town. Everybody knows everybody, and your grandmother was a popular lady."

Enid led Timmy to his bedroom and then brought him a few books on the state's history. "These might be fun to read. I'm going down to check on the coffee pot. They may need a refill."

In light of Jack's earlier revelations about Pratt, just the mention of the name made her nervous. But why would Pratt want to hurt Guinette or Abigail? She went downstairs and put on another pot of coffee and refilled the water kettle for hot tea.

Later, when the meeting was over, Enid went to each person and thanked them for coming. When she saw the woman who had mentioned Abigail was about to leave, Enid rushed over to talk to her. "Hi, I just wanted to thank your club for meeting here. I hope everything was satisfactory."

"Oh, it was wonderful. I'm sure our book club leader will be in touch with you about making this a more permanent arrangement. After all, we need to support local businesses. And, of course, we'll cover the cost of the refreshments and order our books through you."

"I appreciate that. And I agree with you about supporting local businesses. Your husband is the insurance agent, isn't he?"

"Yes, Andy is well-known around here, since he's the only agent." She smiled. "I'll tell him you said hello."

"How long have you lived here? I'm just curious to know more about the town and its residents."

"We moved here a few years ago."

"And where did you come from?" Enid noticed that Mrs. Pratt took a small step backwards.

"We've lived here and there." She looked at her phone. "Oh my, I need to run to an appointment. We'll talk later."

Enid watched as Mrs. Pratt nearly ran down the street in the direction of Andy's office.

CHAPTER 40

Enid and Timmy had just put the last folding chair back in the closet when Josh walked through the door. "Hey, I see you've got a helper."

"I'm the shop assistant," Timmy said.

Josh glanced at Enid. "Oh, excuse me. Shop assistant. That's a nice title there, buddy."

"Would you like a brownie?" Timmy leaned toward Josh and pretended to whisper. "I hid one for you. They were eating them all up."

Josh grinned. "I'd love one. Thanks."

Timmy went behind the counter and pulled out a napkin-wrapped brownie. "Here," he said, handing it to Josh. "I'm reading about Sherman bombing the state house. It's really cool." He ran upstairs.

Enid poured Josh a half cup of coffee. "Sorry, that's all that's left. Want me to make a fresh pot?"

"Nah, this is good." He wiped his mouth with the napkin. "Timmy seems to enjoy helping you."

"I think he needs something to be responsible for. I'll have to give that some thought." She paused and wiped brownie crumbs from the checkout counter. "I need to fill you in on a conversation with Jack." She pointed upstairs. "Let's stay down here."

They settled into the reading chairs and Enid spoke softly. "Were you aware there had been a drug investigation in Blakeley by SLED? It was some kind of a hush-hush thing."

"Not exactly, but when Larkin asked me to look into possible drug trafficking here, he mentioned SLED had done some preliminary poking around, but he didn't want it to be 'official,' so he asked me to quietly look into it. I haven't seen the SLED report."

"What I gathered from Jack is that without the freedom to do an actual investigation, they only found rumors and suspicions that seemed to point to one person."

"I assume you're referring to Miller Blakeley."

"That was my assumption too, but Jack said it was Andy Pratt that SLED focused on."

Josh sat up straight in his chair. "Pratt? The insurance agent?"

Enid nodded. "And guess what? Mrs. Pratt was here with the book club today, and when I asked her about where they lived before moving here, she got very nervous."

"Whew. Now I'm confused. What's going on? And I wonder if the mayor knows about any of this going on in her town?"

"Please don't use Jack's information. We can't put him in that situation."

"I won't. But the governor and I need to have another chat. In the meantime, can you see what you can find out online about Pratt? I'm still not sure who I can trust here, so I'd rather keep this between us for now. I don't want our mayor or anyone else intervening, or even shutting me down."

"Of course. If I can't find anything, I'll get Ginger to help since she has access to all the databases." Enid took Josh's hand in hers. "Jack warned us to be careful. And he said there may be another person involved with Pratt's drug enterprise—someone from out of state."

"That sounds like a bigger operation than just trafficking in Blakeley."

Josh stood. "I'm going to walk down to Pratt's agency and say hello." When he saw Enid's reaction, he held up his palms. "I said just to chat. Nothing more. See you in a bit."

• • •

When Josh walked into the Pratt Insurance Agency, there was no one sitting at the reception desk. "Andy, it's Josh Hart. You here?" Josh heard the sound of a desk drawer closing and then what sounded like a lock engaging.

"Have a seat. I'll be right there."

Josh was barely seated before Pratt came out. "Well, this is a surprise, Chief. You need some insurance? I heard you have a new member of your household."

The hair on Josh's arm tingled at the mention of Timmy, but then he reminded himself there were no secrets in a place as small as Blakeley. "He's just a temporary guest. By the way, did you have a policy on Petula Grant? Her cousin is here to claim the body."

"No, I don't believe so. She has property not far from here, so you might check with them. There's an agent in Orangeburg who writes a lot of rural farm business. He might have written a life policy on her too."

"Thanks, I'll do that." Josh stood as if he were leaving.

"Oh, by the way, your wife mentioned you had moved here from someplace else. I guess I just assumed you had ties here."

"We are proud members of this community and feel like this has always been our home." He appeared to force a smile. "But if you must know, we came from Des Moines."

Josh held up a finger. "Isn't that where your home office is located?"

"We're an independent insurance agent representing a number of companies. That way we can offer our clients the best possible solutions at the best price."

Josh smiled at the sales pitch and pointed to Pratt's many awards on the wall. "But mostly you write for that company. And they're in Des Moines, right?"

Pratt pulled on one of his shirt sleeves. "What is your point, Chief Hart? Or is there a point to all this?"

Josh smiled. "No point, just curious. Just came in to check on Pet's policy. Thanks for the tip, I'll check with the Orangeburg agent." As Josh was walking out the door, he turned back to Pratt. "Must be more business here in Blakeley than I realized. You know, enough to entice you to leave a big city and come here." He smiled. "Thanks again."

CHAPTER 41

Enid was about to close the shop for the day when a woman walked in. "Hi, you must be Mrs. Hart."

"Yes, I'm Josh's wife, Enid Blackwell."

The woman smiled. "Good. I like a woman who keeps her own identity after she marries." She held out her hand. "I'm Meredith, Pet's cousin."

Enid realized she had tensed when the woman walked in. This town was making her jittery—too many secrets. "Hi. Josh said you're here to make arrangements for Pet. I'm so sorry for your loss."

"Thank you." Meredith pointed to one of the chairs. "May I?"

"Of course. Just let me lock the door. I was about to close the shop." Enid turned the ancient lock on the door and pulled the shades down. "Can I get you coffee or tea?"

"Oh, no. I'm sorry to walk in unannounced but something Chief Hart said has been on my mind."

Enid waited for her to continue.

"He said Pet had someone, a young boy, living with her."

"Yes. Timmy. He's upstairs. We don't have any children, so I may not be a good judge, but he seems to be nearly perfect. He's polite, loves school, and is fascinated with books, especially about ghosts and UFOs."

Meredith smiled. "My late husband and I had two daughters, both grown now, of course. One is in California and the other is somewhere in Europe." She shook her head. "I can't keep up with her. Anyway, I was a schoolteacher for about ten years and saw a wide range of students. Some great, and some—well let's just say I was glad to send them home to their parents at the end of the day. But Timmy sounds exceptional. Do you think I could meet him? I don't want to intrude on his life, but if Pet took him in, then he's unofficially part of our family, what's left of it. There're only a few more cousins scattered about. Everyone else has passed on."

Enid mentally raced through all the pros and cons of introducing Timmy to Meredith before answering. How would he react? Would he feel threatened, even though Meredith seemed so warm and kind? "Let me go up and talk to Timmy. If he'd like to meet you, then I'll bring him down. But just remember, he's lost everyone now, and he's afraid we're going to put him in an orphanage. He may see you as a threat."

"I understand."

Enid went upstairs, where Timmy was sitting at his laptop reading about ancient dinosaurs. "Hey. There's a nice lady downstairs who'd like to meet you. She's Pet's cousin." Enid could see the look of confusion in his eyes. "But you don't have to meet her. It's totally your choice."

Timmy shut the laptop. "Will I have to go with her?"

Enid hugged him. "No, honey, it's just to say hello. I promise."

She took Timmy's hand but he pulled away and ran down the stairs ahead of her and stopped at the bottom when he saw Meredith. "Do you miss Pet?" he asked.

Meredith glanced at Enid before responding. "Well, I wish I had spent more time with her. We haven't seen much of each other lately. That's why I didn't know you were staying with her." She motioned to the other chair. "I'd love to hear about your studies. You see, I was a teacher not long ago. Enid says you love school, so tell me about your favorite classes."

Enid relaxed when she saw Timmy smile and sit down beside Meredith. Instead of talking about school, he began chatting away about ghosts, UFOs, dinosaurs, and Sherman's bombing of the South Carolina capitol building. "I'll be upstairs closing out the books for today." She looked at Timmy. "Unless you want me to stay down here."

He shook his head. "I need to tell her about my science project. Maybe she can help me."

Enid was happy they were getting along so well but had a pang of jealousy when Timmy turned to Meredith for help instead of her.

"I'd love to hear about it," Meredith said. "I won't keep him long," she said to Enid.

Enid downloaded the SquareUp transactions for the day and posted them to an Excel file where she tracked the shop's sales and other transactions. When she finished, she went to the top of the stairs and peeked down at Meredith and Timmy, who was still talking away. Enid hoped Timmy wouldn't get too attached. He would likely never see Meredith again once she returned home.

About fifteen minutes later, Meredith called out. "Enid, I'm leaving now. Just wanted to say goodbye."

Enid went downstairs to let her out. "Thanks for

stopping by to meet Timmy. He doesn't get much interaction with others." Enid turned to Timmy. "Why don't you go upstairs while I say goodbye."

Timmy nodded and went running up the stairs. Halfway up, he stopped and turned around. "'Bye, Miss Meredith. Thanks for helping me with my project."

"I want to hear about your grade when you get it. Okay?"

Timmy nodded and ran up the rest of the stairs.

"Please don't befriend him unless you'll stay in touch," Enid said. "He clearly likes you, which is great, but he's desperate for someone to cling to, emotionally, I mean."

Meredith put her hand on Enid's arm. "I understand that. More than you may realize." She walked toward the door. "I need to get back to my room before it's dark. Tomorrow morning, I'm going to the farm to see what needs to be packed and stored or discarded. I'm not one to hold onto family trivia like greeting cards and such, so I'd be surprised if there's much I'll keep. Thanks again for the visit. And you are right. Timmy is nearly perfect."

CHAPTER 42

Armed with a hand-drawn map Josh had given her and a supply of large plastic garbage bags, rubber gloves, and bottles of drinking water from the local Walmart, Meredith headed south down I-26 to the family farm.

Over the years, she had seen a few photos of it but was shocked when she saw how run down the house and barn now looked. She parked in front of the house on the gravel driveway, as an elderly couple emerged from the house to greet her.

"You must be Will and Nellie." Meredith held out her hand. "I'm Meredith, Pet's cousin."

"Chief Hart told us to expect you," Nellie said. "Please come in."

Meredith followed the couple into the small farmhouse, noticing how neat the front lawn and hedges were kept. "You've done a great job keeping the yard up."

"We can't do as much as we used to, but we try to keep the place presentable. At least the outside," Nellie said.

Will spoke for the first time. "I'm not sure about you, but I'm feeling a little awkward about all this."

"Why is that?" Meredith asked.

"This place should rightly be yours. Not sure I feel right about it being left to us."

Meredith laughed. "Then please let me put your mind at ease. Pet and I, unfortunately, were not that close. You know, we did the birthday cards, holiday cards, that kind of thing. I know how long you've been here and how much Pet loved you both. Believe me, I have no interest in owning a farm. It's your home, and you should accept it with the same love Pet had for you. I'm just here to go through the family things she mentioned to see if anything is worth keeping."

"I appreciate you talking straight to us about all this," Will said. "You know, I just didn't want any hard feelings."

"See, Will, I told you it would all be fine," Nellie said. "Come on, Meredith, I'll show you the personal things. I put everything in that one back bedroom that's empty. And I may have put a few things in the attic.

"I've got to do some work in the barn," Will said. "Come get one of us if you need anything. I'll show you those attic stairs, but you be careful going up and down."

Will showed Meredith where the pull-down access door was located in the hallway and then he and Nellie left Meredith alone in the house.

There were at least a dozen medium sized boxes stacked in the middle of the back bedroom. None of them were labeled as to contents. Meredith pulled up a wooden chair by the window and began going through the nearest box.

• • •

A couple hours later, Nellie brought in a sandwich and a cup of soup. "I figured you'd want to keep working, but if you'd rather come to the dining room, I'll set you up there."

"Oh, no. This is fine. Thanks. And I've got some water here, so I don't need anything else."

"Looks like you're making good progress on those boxes," Nellie said.

Meredith held up an old Montblanc fountain pen. "So far, this is the only thing I've found worth keeping. I remember Pet saying her father always wrote with a pen like this, so I assume it was his. Do you have a place we can dump all the rest? I've made a stack of the papers to be shredded. I can take those back with me."

"Will can load up those boxes and all the other stuff and take it to the landfill if you want." She pointed to a stack of papers. "We got a shredder Will bought, so we can do that too. You been in the attic yet?"

"No, I need to finish these last couple of boxes and then I'll tackle that."

"Just put aside anything you want to take with you. Anything else you leave, we'll dispose of." Nellie laughed. "Pet was a bit of a pack rat."

"I can't tell you how much I appreciate your help. Without being too nosy, can I ask what your plans are for the farm?"

"Will wants to grow herbs, of all things. He says there's a big market for 'em."

"Well, I know how much I pay for fresh herbs at the store, so he's probably right."

Nellie nodded. "And we'll keep raising pygmy goats 'cause they bring a pretty penny. The eggs we sell are just pocket money. If you don't need anything else, I'll leave you now."

An hour later, Meredith climbed up the attic stairs to see what was there. She was soon covered in dust and was getting tired. Maybe she'd have to come back tomorrow to finish. Reluctantly, she poked around in a few of the things to see what she was dealing with. More old papers and junk, she assumed. But she found some old photos and other family mementos worth keeping. This was beginning to look like a two-day project. She decided to go through one more box before going down to tell Nellie and Will she'd have to come back and finish tomorrow.

Most of the boxes were weathered and a few were damaged by moisture from an apparent roof leak. But one box looked newer than the others, and it was a banker's box, the kind used to store documents, rather than the odd assortment of cardboard boxes the rest of the things had been packed in.

Meredith opened the box. Inside was an envelope addressed to Pet. It was unopened, sealed shut. She put it aside to look at the remaining contents. A thumb drive and some photos that looked like a young couple with a small child. The inscription on the back, written in pencil, was two names and then "Timmy." The box also contained several years' worth of hand-written journals.

The single-bulb light in the attic was losing the battle against the encroaching darkness. Meredith pushed the box to the edge and then eased herself down the ladder a few steps. "Will, are you there?" She heard footsteps then a voice.

"Yes, ma'am. You need something?"

"Can you help me get this box down? I'm going to take it with me."

Meredith carefully made her way down the ladder until

192 · RAEGAN TELLER

she was on the floor again, and then Will retrieved the box. For his age, he appeared to be unusually strong and had no problem getting the box down or navigating the ladder. "You want this in the room?"

"I'd like to take it with me if you don't mind putting it in my car."

After Will took the box outside, Meredith thanked Nellie again for the lunch and for their hospitality. She promised to come back the next day to finish.

By the time Meredith was back on the highway to her hotel, it was dark and beginning to rain. She didn't like to drive after dark, especially when she was unfamiliar with an area. Normally, she wouldn't have paid attention to the headlights behind her, but given all that had happened, she was uneasy. She pressed the voice command button on her phone, "Siri, call Josh Hart mobile."

When the call went to voice mail, Meredith glanced at the rear mirror again. She couldn't be sure, but it looked like the same car was still following her. "This is Meredith. I'm leaving the farm, and I'm not sure but someone may be following me. Call me when you get this."

After she got off the state road and onto I-26 again, she relaxed a bit. But the car followed her and was even closer. When her cell phone rang, she jumped. "Hello."

"It's Josh. Where are you?"

She gave him the last mile marker she had seen.

"I know about where you are. Put your flashers on and keep driving. When you get to your hotel exit, I should be there. I'm leaving now."

CHAPTER 43

Josh gave Enid a quick peck on the cheek. "Gotta go. Be back when I can."

"Is everything okay?"

"I hope so. I'm going to meet Meredith. Someone may be following her."

"Call me when you can and let me know she's safe."

"Will do," Josh said as he jogged down the stairs and out the door.

Timmy came out of his room. "Where's Josh going?"

Enid gave him a hug. "He's going to do some police work. We'll have to eat without him. Would you like some soup?"

Timmy nodded.

"Good. I'll heat some and bring you a tray. Would that be okay with you?" The look on Timmy's face was answer enough. "Alright, we'll have a bowl together, but then I've got some work to do."

Timmy's face lit up with a smile. "Can we have a peanut butter and jelly sandwich with it?"

"Of course." The combination reminded Enid of her own elementary school days when vegetable soup and a peanut butter sandwich were standard fare at least once a week, mostly Fridays.

After the meal, Timmy went off to this room and Enid went to the small desk in their bedroom that was her makeshift office. A far cry from her office at the bank years ago in Charlotte. Even her office at the *Tri-County Gazette* in Madden was spacious compared to this tiny portion of the room she claimed for work.

She texted Ginger and got her login info for several databases, including Ancestry.com. Not having much to go on, she had low expectations of finding out more about Timmy's family. She knew his parents' names from the newspaper articles she found about their tragic accident. After twenty minutes or so, she found a female who could be related. She jotted down the name of the woman whose address was in Tennessee, at least at one time. Another search revealed a phone number.

She reached for her phone but stopped. Unsure why she was hesitating, she began to tap in the numbers. Before the last number, she stopped. What if they were horrible people and wanted to claim Timmy? What if they claimed they were related but really weren't? Enid stood up and stretched, talking to herself out loud. *"Okay, Enid, admit it. You've grown fond of Timmy. But you're not the maternal type. And he needs to be with real family. You are, or at least you were, an investigative reporter, for Pete's sake. You know how to check people out."* Pushing her doubts aside, she called the number. After a few rings, a woman answered.

"Hi, I'm Enid Blackwell. I run a bookstore and coffee shop in Blakeley, South Carolina. I'm trying to find relatives for Timmy Sullivan." There was a long silence at the other end. "Hello? Are you still there?"

"Is Abigail . . . Did she . . . ?"

Enid could hear the distress in the woman's voice. "I'm

MURDER CLAUSE · 195

sorry but Abigail died recently. Are you related to her?"

The woman gasped. "I'm sorry to hear that. We grew apart after a silly argument, and I haven't talked to her in years. Oh, God. What about Timmy? Where is he now? Abigail was all he had."

"How are you related to Abigail?"

"She was my aunt. My mother was a dreadful person, and, God rest her soul, convinced all of us that Abigail was the reason our dad left, you know, to be with Abigail. But none of that was true. And shamefully, once I found out the truth, I was too embarrassed to apologize to Abigail."

Enid heard the woman crying softly.

"But Timmy? Where is he?"

"I'm afraid I can't give you that information over the phone. My husband, Josh Hart, is the chief of police in Blakeley, and I'll have him contact you."

In a soft voice so low, it was nearly inaudible, the woman said, "I understand. Yes, please have him contact me."

"Are you married?"

"Yes. My husband and I live just outside of Nashville." She laughed softly. "But of course, you know where I am or you couldn't have found me. I look forward to hearing from Chief Hart. But can you tell me if Timmy is hurt or anything?"

"He's doing great, all things considered. He's a good kid."

"I haven't seen him since he was a baby."

Enid wanted to tell her more but decided caution was the best approach. "We'll be in touch. Thank you."

. . .

Josh parked in a small, cleared area beside the road. Nearly fifteen minutes later, he saw a car in the exit lane with flashers on. He flashed his headlights and when she was close, he pulled into the Mobile gas store just down from the exit, parking near the back. Meredith pulled in and parked beside him.

A large black SUV pulled in behind Meredith but then sped away quickly. Josh was unable to get a license number. But he didn't need it because he knew that vehicle well. Miller Blakeley.

Josh got out of the car and walked to the driver's side of Meredith's vehicle. "You okay?"

Meredith nodded. "Did you see him? He was right behind me all the way."

"I saw him. When did he start following you?"

"I'm not sure exactly, but it was soon after I left the farm. Why would someone follow me? I don't know anyone around here."

"But they apparently know you're connected to Pet somehow. Follow me. You can stay with us tonight. Timmy wanted a sleeping bag, so we got him one. He's been anxious to try it out."

"Are you sure? I don't want to put anyone out."

"Until I can check out your follower, I don't feel good about leaving you alone."

"By the way, I found a box of Abigail's things in Pet's attic. There's a letter to Pet also, but I haven't read it."

"We'll check it out when we get to the shop. Just follow

close behind me."

On the way home, Josh phoned Enid and told her Meredith was fine and coming to stay for the night.

"And I found one of Timmy's relatives," Enid said. "I'll fill you in when you get here."

• • •

As Josh predicted, Timmy was excited about trying out his new sleeping bag. Enid gave him an old tote bag to use as a backpack on his imaginary adventure. He insisted on sleeping in the kitchen area.

While Timmy was setting up camp in front of the stove, Josh suggested they go downstairs to talk. Enid told him about finding a possible relative, and then Meredith produced the letter she had found.

"Somehow I feel like I'm intruding by opening this. I mean, it's not really addressed to me."

Josh reached for the letter. "Under the circumstances, I'd say it's police business." He pulled out a typed page.

Dear Pet,

If you're reading this, well, then things might not have gone as planned. When I gave you this box to store for me, I decided to add this letter. I didn't say anything because I hoped I was just being paranoid, and I didn't want to scare you. But here's what you need to know.

Guinette was convinced Miller was going to kill her. She confronted him about stealing money from her personal account and threatened to turn him in if he didn't shut down the airstrip and walk away from his drug dealings. I made copies of her business accounts and put them on the flash drive in the box in case Miller tried to change anything later—or destroy everything.

During the past few weeks, I've seen bruises on Guinette's neck and arm where he attacked her. So I made arrangements for her to leave the area and stay upstate in a remote area in a friend's cabin. I also promised her I'd set up a meeting for her with SLED. She was more determined than ever to turn Miller in and reclaim a life she could be proud of.

But then I found her dead in her bed. An intentional overdose of Fentanyl-laced drugs, brought on by depression. Or so they said. But I never once saw her take anything stronger than Tylenol. And she hated illegal drugs. She wasn't depressed—just angry and scared.

After she died, Miller fired me. No surprise, and I had no reason to stay anyway. But now I'm afraid for me and Timmy. Andy Pratt came to see me. He told me I needed to mind my own business and not to make things any worse for "poor Miller," who had just lost his wife. I told him if anything happened to me, facts would come to light. I've never liked Andy very much, and now I'm scared of him too. That look in his eyes. I'll never forget it.

So I'm going to start looking for a place for me and Timmy far away from here, away from Blakeley. This place is full of secrets and sin. I feel guilty that I couldn't have done something to save Guinette. I should have gone to the police myself. I'll have to live with that. And I have nothing to prove Miller or one of his drug buddies killed her. But I know they did. What's in this box, though, will show how he stole from Guinette's personal account. Maybe it will help put him away. I pray it does.

When Timmy is old enough to understand, you can give him my journals and explain all this.

Love,
Abigail

For a few seconds, no one said anything. Josh folded the letter and returned it to the envelope. Enid was the first to speak. "We've got to do something. Miller can't get away with this."

Meredith shifted her weight in the chair. "Is this why Pet was killed? Because she knew all this?"

Josh sat with the letter in his hands, staring at it. "I don't think Pet was aware of this information, or she would have told me. But it does sound like I need to pay another visit to our local insurance agent." He turned to Meredith. "And I'd like to know why Miller was following you."

Enid put her hand on Josh's arm. "Maybe it's time to let SLED take this case. Three people are already dead."

"You may be right. But first, I need to talk to my boss."

"The mayor?" Enid asked.

"No, Governor Larkin."

CHAPTER 44

When Josh arrived at the governor's home in Columbia, where Larkin insisted they meet, he was shown in immediately and taken to a private office at the rear of the large mansion. "Come on in, Josh. Good to see you." Larkin shut the heavy oak door and gestured toward a large antique console table. "We've got coffee over here, or something stronger if you prefer."

"I'm good, thanks." Josh paused to gather his thoughts. "I'm not going to beat around the bush. I think Miller Blakeley killed his wife Guinette, or perhaps had her killed. Your investigator said as much." He paused and glanced at the painting of John Rutledge, who was elected as South Carolina's first governor in 1776. Josh had seen the painting on previous visits but today it somehow made him acutely aware of the gravity of speaking to the top politician in the state. If this meeting went downhill, he and Enid would have to make some quick decisions. And if Larkin was somehow involved, even if it was only overlooking Miller Blakeley's crimes, their life in South Carolina would be over.

Pushing those thoughts aside, Josh now studied Larkin's face. Unlike the portrait of Rutledge, Larkin was alive and present, sitting no more than three feet away. "And he may have played a part in the death of Abigail Sullivan." Josh decided not to mention Pet just yet.

"Those are some serious accusations. But I'm sure you're

aware of that." His typical smile had faded. "You're a smart man." He laughed. "And you're not a politician. I think you made that perfectly clear the last time we worked together. But you know how to do the political tango when you have to."

Josh repositioned himself in the chair. The upholstery was deep and soft, making it difficult to sit up straight for very long. "I'm not here to tango. I want to know what you intend to do, so I don't step on your toes." Josh cleared his throat. "But I will pursue this, even if you don't."

Larkin took a sip of whiskey from a heavy crystal glass. "I see. So are you here to threaten me, ask for my advice, or . . . Just why are you here?"

"You asked me to investigate, quietly, any possible drug trafficking in Blakeley. You said the town's proximity to I-95 made it a transportation hub for dealers. But you knew all along that one of your major campaign contributors was likely involved. And you knew I'd find out. Was your plan to get me to go after Miller so your hands would be clean? And then what? Get the charges thrown out for insufficient evidence?"

The muscles in Larkin's jaw tightened. "You must have a pretty low opinion of me." He relaxed his face and smiled slightly. "Or perhaps you don't trust any politicians. Not sure I can blame you. There aren't many I trust either. But the fact is this, Josh. I asked you to investigate with an open mind. I wanted to see what you would uncover. Yes, Miller is an old friend and a loyal contributor. But if, and I do mean *if,* you can prove his involvement in drug trafficking or worse yet, murder, then he will be prosecuted. You'll have to trust me on that."

"I'm glad to hear you say that, and I'll take you at your word. But you kept my assignment off the books, and it's now time to make it official and bring in SLED. I don't have to remind you how limited our small town's resources are." Josh glanced at Rutledge's portrait again. "And I'm afraid my family and I may be in danger."

"I'll talk to the SLED chief. He'll contact you to get whatever you have. But I warn you, once you've opened this gate, there's no closing it."

And if I can't prove anything, I'm the one in trouble. "I want to talk to Andy Pratt this afternoon. I'll need that information before SLED takes over."

"Andy? You haven't mentioned him as being involved."

Foolishly, Josh had not considered that the governor and Andy might be friends. "That's what I believe, sir. And there's someone else who's running the operation. I believe Miller and Andy are only players. But I believe you were aware Pratt had been the target of an earlier, covert investigation, since you ordered it."

Larkin stood, a sign the meeting was over. "Keep me posted and tell me when you want me to make that call."

CHAPTER 45

Meredith offered to spend the day with Timmy to help him with his science project. Enid wasn't sure which one of them was more excited. While they were working in Timmy's room, Enid went downstairs to unpack and then record and shelve some new books that had come in.

She was on her knees dusting the edges of the bottom shelves when the bell on the door signaled someone had entered. She stood up and brushed the dust from her jeans before looking up. "I'll be right with you."

When the visitor didn't answer, Enid looked to see who it was, and they locked eyes. "Hello, Ms. Blackwell. Sorry to disturb you."

Enid took a deep breath to steady her nerves. "Mr. Pratt, what a pleasant surprise. How can I help you?"

"I was just hoping to find Chief Hart. He wasn't at the police station just now."

"I'm sorry, but he's not here. You can leave a message at the station and they'll have him call you. I try to stay out of his work."

"Thanks. And by the way, is that boy still staying with you?"

Enid brushed her jeans again. "Why do you ask?"

"I know someone who's looking for a child about his age to foster."

"We're taking care of all that. Now, is there anything else

I can help you with?" She forced a smile.

Andy's cold stare made him look like a wax figure. "No. Thanks for your time."

After he left, Enid sat in one of the chairs and tried to steady her shaking hands. She left a message for Josh to call her immediately and then went upstairs where Meredith and Timmy were working. When she got to the top of the stairs, she heard Timmy laughing. Enid tapped on the door. "Sounds like you two are having too much fun to be studying."

Meredith turned from the laptop to face Enid. "We were laughing at . . . well, it's not important." Timmy giggled at the image on the screen.

"Can I talk with you just a minute?" Enid asked Meredith.

"Of course." Meredith turned to Timmy. "Why don't you read about the wee folk of Ireland, and we'll include them in your project if you'd like."

Enid motioned for Meredith to follow her. "Wee folk?"

Meredith smiled. "Timmy is doing a project on folklore. He has such a natural curiosity about everything, especially anything supernatural or mysterious. It's so refreshing. Speaking of supernatural, you look like you've seen a ghost."

Enid told Meredith about Andy Pratt's visit. "I think he's going to turn us in."

"But you've notified the authorities about Timmy, right?"

Enid shook her head. "I promised him he wouldn't have to go to a foster home. And now I'm afraid Pratt is going to force the issue."

"You need to file that report right away and request guardianship. I'll help you."

Enid nodded.

Meredith cocked her head slightly. "Or do you not want to be his guardian?"

"I've never seen myself as a mother."

"And now?"

"Timmy is an amazing child. But becoming a guardian is a big step. I want to do what's right for everyone involved."

"What does Josh think?"

"I think he'd agree if I wanted to. But there is a relative. We need to check her out. In the meantime, can you keep Timmy in your sight? I need to go to the police station, and I want to be sure he's safe."

"Of course. Is there anything I can do?"

"I don't think so. I'll be back shortly, but I'm going to close the shop."

. . .

Enid grabbed her tote bag and ran down the stairs. Just as she was headed to the door, Josh walked in. She grabbed him and threw her arms around his neck. "I'm so glad to see you."

"What's going on? Your message sounded urgent."

"Andy Pratt came here. He was looking for you. And he has someone who wants to foster Timmy. We've got to request guardianship."

"Whoa. One thing at a time. You gave me the name of a relative, and I've checked her out. No criminal record, and she appears legit."

"I checked her out too, and I agree she seems to be legit. But Timmy doesn't know her, and I promised him he wouldn't go into foster care."

Josh sighed. "Let's call her before we jump to any conclusions."

They sat in the two reading chairs, and Josh tapped in the phone number Enid had given him. "Ms. Parker, this is Chief Joshua Hart in Blakeley, South Carolina. I'm calling to follow up on a conversation you had with my wife about Timmy."

Josh explained the situation to Ms. Parker. "I understand. Yes, I'll keep you posted. Thanks for your time."

Enid leaned forward in her chair. "What did she say?"

"She's sympathetic to Timmy's situation but doesn't want to be his guardian. Apparently, she's having health issues and can't commit."

"That doesn't leave us much choice. We'll have to become his guardians."

"Are you sure?" Josh asked. "I know he's a great kid and all that, but are we ready for this?"

"He's also a smart kid, and he needs to be in this conversation."

"I'm not sure that's a good idea. He's a bit young to be deciding his own future." He paused and ran his hand through his hair. "But I don't have a better idea."

"Let's go upstairs to the dining table." Enid locked the shop door and turned the sign around to show "closed."

Josh sat at the table and Enid went to ask Timmy to join them.

"Would you like for me to leave?" Meredith asked. "If this is a family discussion, then I don't need to intrude."

"No, you have to come too," Timmy said, grabbing Meredith's hand.

Another pang of jealousy gripped Enid, and then she silently chastised herself for being petty. "Of course you can join us."

When they were all seated, Timmy was the first one to speak. "Am I in trouble?"

Enid reached out and took his small hand in hers. "No, honey. We just want to tell you what's going on." She glanced at Josh and then Meredith, before turning back to Timmy. "We need to tell the authorities that you're here. You see, we need to file for guardianship before we all get into trouble."

"What does that mean? Am I going to have to leave?" Timmy asked.

"We're going to ask them to let you stay here."

"Forever?" Timmy asked.

"Until we figure out the best place for you, and what you want to do," Enid said.

Timmy turned to Meredith. "Can you visit me some more?"

Meredith smiled. "Of course. And you could stay with me for a while if Josh and Enid are okay with that. I have a nice place near the mountains."

Timmy nodded vigorously.

"I'd like to make a suggestion," Josh said. "Timmy, can you go work on your project while we talk about this? I promise you we'll let you know what's going on." Josh glanced at Enid. "And I promise we'll make sure you have a good home."

Timmy nodded, his young face reflecting the uncertainty he was likely feeling.

When Timmy was out of earshot, Josh and Meredith started to speak at the same time and both laughed. "You first," Josh said.

Meredith put her hand on Enid's arm. "I only want what's best for Timmy. He's an exceptional child. If I had a son, I'd want him to be like Timmy." She paused. "But I'm not going to get into a tug-of-war with you. You've both been wonderful to provide him with a home."

"What are you saying? Do you want to foster Timmy?" Enid asked.

Meredith nodded. "But only if you don't want to take him."

Josh looked at Enid. "This may be the best solution. Unless you're ready to be a mother." He turned to Meredith. "Are you prepared for this to be a permanent solution?"

She smiled. "I think so. Actually, I'm surprised myself, but I'd love to have him as a son."

Enid clapped. "I know Timmy would love that. You have a special way with him. But we need to get that petition filed right away before Andy pulls some kind of stunt."

Josh stood up. "I'll let you two work on that. I've got to pay a visit to our friend Miller Blakeley."

CHAPTER 46

Josh walked up the steps to the Blakeley mansion, his second visit to the palatial residence of Miller and the late Guinette Blakeley. The last time, he was greeted by a woman, presumably a maid or some kind of assistant, so he expected her to open the door. When no one answered, he rang the doorbell again and could hear the melodious chimes announce his presence. But no one came to the door, so he used the giant doorknocker in the shape of a palmetto tree. On the second knock, the door gave way and opened slightly.

Josh backed up and studied the large door. There was no sign of it being jimmied or damaged in any way. He pushed the door open a little further. "Hello. Anyone here?"

Josh pulled the door shut and followed the gravel walkway to the back of the house. A large glass atrium full of green plants came into view. Next to it, the back door was standing wide open. Instinctively, Josh put his hand on the 9mm Glock in its holster as he stepped inside. "This is Chief Hart. Anybody here?"

The small mudroom had a black and white tiled floor and hooks on the wall. A yellow rubber Mackintosh raincoat hung on one of them. Another door led from the mudroom to the kitchen. Josh pushed the door open slightly. "Hello. Anybody here?"

As soon as he pushed the door open, he saw the red

puddle spreading from behind the wide island in the middle of the kitchen. Josh pulled his gun and walked inside. After a quick look around, he walked back outside and radioed his deputy. "Come over here and notify the sheriff to send a crime scene unit. We've got a body." He then heard what sounded like a small airplane engine. It was coming from the direction of the small landing strip not far from the house.

The next call Josh made was to Governor Larkin. "It's time to call in SLED. Miller is dead."

· · ·

Within minutes, Officer Holden showed up and he and Josh searched the house and grounds but found no one or any indications of what may have happened.

"What about that plane you heard take off?" Holden asked. "Should we see if they filed a flight plan?"

"Private planes are not required to file a flight plan unless they are flying into restricted airspace. But if whoever left here plans to fly a long distance, the FAA might have something. Why don't you check it out?"

When the sheriff's office crime scene investigator arrived, she began processing all the rooms for prints and other evidence. "Your little town is becoming a hotbed of crime, it seems," she said.

Josh smiled. "It appears so. Just to let you know, I've requested the governor send in SLED. They may show up here later."

"Thanks for the heads up."

A few minutes later, Officer Holden walked up to Josh,

a big grin across his face. "Bingo."

"What did you find out?" Josh asked.

"A private plane leaving from a private airport here in Orangeburg County filed a last-minute flight plan to a small airport in Georgia."

"Might not be related to any of this," Josh said.

"Or it might be. The pilot is Andy Pratt."

. . .

Before the scene had been fully processed, a black SUV emblazoned with South Carolina Law Enforcement Division arrived at Blakeley's house. Josh introduced himself to Officer Goodwin and told him what he knew about the case. He also told him about the small plane that took off. When he mentioned Andy Pratt's name, Josh thought he noticed a twitch in the SLED officer's jaw.

"Thanks for the update, Chief Hart. That's what you know. Now what do you suspect but can't prove?"

Josh liked this guy. "We've had three, now it's four, deceased that all seem to be connected somehow. I thought Miller Blakeley was responsible directly or indirectly for the death of his wife Guinette. He may have also been involved in the alleged accidental fall that killed Abigail Sullivan. And Pet, the thrift shop owner died as a result of injuries sustained in her abduction. I'm still trying to piece it all together, but as I told Governor Larkin, our resources are very limited here."

"Sounds like you've done a good job with what you had to work with. I'll keep you in the loop." He turned back to

Josh as he was walking away. "And just to let you know, Pratt's been on our radar ever since he moved here. But we never had enough to go after him."

"I hear he's a friend of Larkin."

"Yeah, there's that too."

CHAPTER 47

Meredith sat down with Timmy in his room. "I want to ask you something, and I want you to tell me the truth. Okay?"

Timmy nodded.

"If we can get permission, would you like to come live with me?"

"You mean forever?"

Meredith smiled. "Well, I think that depends on what you want to do." She took his small hands in hers. "Enid and Josh have been good to you, and I know you like them a lot. So if you'd rather stay here, they said you can stay as long as you like. But either way, we have to tell social services about your situation. Do you understand that?"

Timmy's eyes filled with tears. "But what if they put me in an orphanage?"

Meredith squeezed his small hands gently. "We won't let that happen. Too many people love you and will fight for you. Understand?"

Timmy wiped the tears on his sleeve and nodded. "Will I have my own room?"

"Of course. And I've been thinking of getting this little farm. Wouldn't that be fun?"

Timmy jumped up and put his arms around Meredith's neck. "Can we visit Enid and Josh?"

"Of course. They can come visit us too. So I've got to go make some phone calls. I promise to let you know what's going on."

"Will you keep teaching me?"

"Yes, I'd love to. There's so much we can learn together."

Timmy nodded. "Thank you."

Meredith blinked away her tears and said a silent prayer that she could get guardianship without too much hassle or delay. Government agencies work notoriously slow and sometimes have arbitrary rules that aren't always in the child's best interest.

When Meredith walked downstairs, Enid was sitting with a woman. "Oh, Meredith, I'd like for you to meet Ruby-Grace Murray. She goes by Roo for short."

"Hi, Roo, I've heard about you. Glad to finally meet you."

"How did the meeting with Timmy go?" Enid asked.

Meredith grinned. "Great. He's excited but made me promise you'd come to visit us."

Roo said to Enid, "Well, I guess you missed your chance at being a mother."

Enid sighed. "I admit, it was tempting, but when I see him with Meredith, I know we've all made the right decision. And, yes, we'll definitely continue to be in his life if he wants us."

"Good. But I'll need some letters of reference. Do you think you and Josh could do that? I'll get letters from the people who know me at home. I've got some solid contacts there."

"Of course, but Josh is tied up for a while."

"Yeah, Miller Blakeley finally met his maker," Roo said.

"Wish I could feel sorry for him. When I heard the news, I had to come back here and make sure it was true. I won't ask if there are any suspects, because I know you couldn't say even if you knew."

"I only talked briefly to Josh. He said SLED was involved and would likely take over the investigation."

"Just as well," Roo said.

"I'm going to go up and get started on the guardian application," Meredith said.

After Meredith went upstairs, Roo leaned in and spoke softly. "Are you sure about all this? I mean I saw how much you care for Timmy."

Enid smiled. "Believe me, I've thought about it a lot. But I've never wanted to be a mother. I love Timmy, but he needs someone like Meredith. She's had parenting experience, and she's a retired schoolteacher and does tutoring online. And Timmy is like a sponge. He loves to study. They're a perfect fit for each other. I just hope she can get approved as his guardian."

"So what will you do now? Will Josh be persona non grata in Blakeley after investigating Miller?"

"All I know is the mayor came by here looking for him. She didn't look too happy."

"But what about your happiness? I can't picture you running this little shop, charming as it is, until you're old and gray. You're too smart to wither away in Blakeley."

Enid shrugged. "Josh and I will have to figure that out."

Roo looked around the shop. "Yeah, right."

CHAPTER 48

The crime scene investigator called Josh aside. "Before I tell SLED, just wanted you to know we got a good footprint that doesn't match the victim's shoes. The shoe's an Italian loafer, so hopefully we can connect it to someone."

"Thanks, I appreciate the update." Josh motioned toward Goodwin who was walking toward them. "Speaking of SLED."

"Pratt's office says he left unexpectedly," Goodwin said. "We'll bring him in for questioning."

"Maybe he's the one who belongs to the Italian loafer," the CSI tech said. She told Goodwin about the print. "I checked the SoleMate database. Santoni brand."

"Excellent. Get me anything you've got."

"Will do. I'll finish up and file my report." The crime scene tech walked back to the kitchen area where the body had been found.

When she was gone, Josh rubbed his neck to get out the stiffness and said to Goodwin, "Sounds like you want it to be Pratt. Or am I imagining that?"

Goodwin laughed. "Spot on. He's smart enough to have gotten away with a lot, but even the smart ones eventually screw up."

"You think Pratt killed Miller, but what about Guinette? Why would he kill her?"

"Simple. We've suspected for years that Pratt and Miller

were partners in crime, but for various reasons we weren't given the green light to go after them. Sounds like you've gotten a taste of what that's like while working with Larkin. We knew Pratt and Miller were in the drug trafficking business, and I think they were also partners in murder. You see, I think Pratt talked Miller into taking out a big insurance policy on Guinette, probably laying the groundwork for her eventual murder. When Pratt found out later that Miller desperately needed money, he probably suggested they kill her and split the money. There's some unsubstantiated buzz that Pratt has set up this kind of thing before, in another state."

"Who do you think actually killed Guinette?" Josh asked.

"I think we'll find that Pratt was the actual killer. I'm sure Miller was more than happy to let him do the dirty work."

"And Abigail Sullivan?"

"We haven't tied him to her death yet or to the thrift shop lady."

"I think I can fill in some of the blanks. Whoever killed Abigail must have known or suspected she left some documentation. After all, she was an administrative assistant, and they're prone to taking detailed notes." As far as Petula Grant, she was Abigail's best friend and Abigail confided in her. Abigail also left materials at Pet's farm for safe keeping that implicated Miller in several crimes. We've found some of the information, and there may be more. According to Abigail, Miller was allegedly involved in drug trafficking and stole money from Guinette's personal accounts. So after Abigail's death, I think Miller went after Pet to get the incriminating documents and destroy them."

"I'll need whatever you've found."

"Of course, but some of it is in Abigail's personal journals. I'd like for Timmy to get her journals, which was her request."

"We'll have to go through all the material from Sullivan and see if it has any evidentiary value. We can pull what we need and get the rest back to the boy." He shook his head. "Damn shame." He paused. "We're looking for Pratt now. I'll let you know when we've got him. I mean, you've done most of the legwork, so I thought you might want in on the finale.

"Absolutely. Wouldn't miss it."

· · ·

Enid was surprised when Mrs. Pratt walked into the bookstore. In fact, she was one of the last people Enid expected to see considering their last conversation. "Mrs. Pratt. This is a surprise."

Mrs. Pratt looked out the front window, glancing up and down the street as if looking for someone. "I need to talk to you. Privately."

The alarms went off in Enid's mind. What was Mrs. Pratt up to? Had her husband sent her here? But the reporter in her wanted to know what Mrs. Pratt had to say. "Have a seat." Enid walked to the door and locked it, flipping the "open" sign over. "Let me turn off my phone so we won't be disturbed." But instead, Enid hit the record icon and hid the phone slightly behind a stack of books on the table beside the chair. "How can I help you?"

"You were a reporter, right?"

"I was, but I'm not any longer."

Mrs. Pratt played with a tissue in her hand. Enid noticed her eyes were slightly swollen, and there appeared to be a bruise under her right eye showing through a heavy layer of makeup.

"Are you alright?" Enid asked. "Can I get you a cup of tea or coffee?"

Mrs. Pratt shook her head. "Could you write about me and my son?"

"I'm sorry, I don't understand. As I said, I'm no longer a reporter."

"But you could, with your contacts, right?" Tears filled Mrs. Pratt's eyes.

Enid leaned forward. "Why don't you just tell me what's going on, and then I'll tell you if I can help."

Mrs. Pratt pulled at the tissue again. "I remember reading your stories. You seemed to care about the people, not just the crime. I also remember you being quoted as saying you were a journalist because you wanted to find the truth."

"That's true." Enid paused. "Are you in some kind of trouble?"

Mrs. Pratt shook her head. "I don't know, but Andy is. He left the country today. I think because something awful has happened. But he wouldn't tell me."

"Are you saying he's left for good? Without you and your son?"

"My son is from a previous marriage." She smiled slightly. "He's a good boy. I married Andy so my son could have a father after my husband died of pancreatic cancer." She dabbed at her eyes with what was left of the tissue. "At first, Andy was good to us. He makes a lot of money, so we had everything we wanted. But then, he went to work for *that* company and we were sent here."

"You mean the insurance company?"

Mrs. Pratt nodded. "That man, Nathan Adams, I know he's behind all this. I never liked him. And now I'm worried about my son and what people will say."

"Say about what?"

Mrs. Pratt looked around the bookstore. "I envy you. You seem to have the ideal life here." She paused and looked around again. "But you have to promise me you'll tell our side of the story. Tell people my son's real father was a military veteran, a good man. My son deserves a better life than what Andy has given us. Andy has ruined our reputation."

"Mrs. Pratt, I want to help you, I really do. But as I said, I'm not a reporter. But I'll be glad to get some information from you and then I'll ask a friend of mine to write your story. Jack Johnson manages the *Tri-County Gazette,* but he's got contacts at the *State,* the *Post and Courier,* and the other dailies throughout the state. He can make sure your story is published."

Mrs. Pratt nodded. "Thank you."

"But I also need to tell you that I'll have to share whatever you tell me with my husband, Chief Hart. I can't keep this information from him."

"I understand."

"May I record this conversation so I can get the details right?"

When Mrs. Pratt agreed, Enid stopped the previous recording and started a new one. "This is Enid Blackwell, and

I'm interviewing Mrs.—I'm sorry, what's your first name?"

"Bernadette."

"I'm interviewing Bernadette Pratt, wife of Andy Pratt, who is the local insurance agent in Blakeley, South Carolina."

For the next fifteen minutes, Mrs. Pratt spoke mostly about her husband's suspicious behavior and about the "odd" Mr. Adams, who was Andy's sales manager at Foster Insurance. Enid was afraid there wasn't much of a story because there were few facts. But then Mrs. Pratt said, "I overheard Andy telling Mr. Adams on the phone that he would make sure Abigail Sullivan didn't talk."

Enid sat up straight in her chair. "Are you saying your husband . . .?"

"I'm saying I heard him tell his boss that he would 'eliminate' Ms. Sullivan to keep her quiet. He talked about throwing her down the stairs."

Enid checked her phone to be sure it was still recording and wished Josh were here. "Did he mention Petula Grant, the owner of the thrift shop next door?"

"No, I never heard him mention her name, but the night she was attacked, he came home and called Mr. Adams to tell him 'everything was taken care of.' Of course, Andy didn't know I was listening to his calls. If he had known, he would probably have killed me too."

"I have to ask. Did you have anything to do with these attacks?" Enid asked.

Mrs. Pratt stiffened. "No, of course not. That's why I'm here talking to you. He's ruined our family, and I'm so ashamed. I want you to tell people who we really are, my son

222 · RAEGAN TELLER

and I."

"Why didn't you just go to the police?"

"I was afraid, for me and my son. Andy is a mean person and I know what he's capable of. All he wants is money and power." She lowered her head. "He's not the person I thought I married. When he left us today to deal with all this on our own, I knew I had to talk to someone."

"Do you know where he's gone?" Enid asked.

"No, but I saw a deed once in his office, in a name I didn't recognize, to a house in Brazil. He may have gone there."

Enid didn't say anything but was relieved to hear Pratt may have gone to a country with an extradition agreement with the US. Maybe they could find him and bring him back for trial. "Where can I reach you if I need more information?"

"I'm not sure where my son and I will go. He's with a friend of mine now. It's not safe to stay at our house. I'll contact you again later."

"Let's take you to the police station, so you can give an official report." Enid reached out and took Mrs. Pratt's hand in hers. "Everything will be fine. You're free of him now."

CHAPTER 49

Enid and Bernadette walked into the small Blakeley police station looking for Josh. The dispatcher said he was on a call but would be in soon. "Can we wait in his office?" Enid asked. "We need to talk to him right away."

"That's fine."

As Enid and Mrs. Pratt walked into Josh's office, the dispatcher followed them in. "Josh is on his way in now, and I told him you were here. He's with that SLED officer."

A few minutes later, Josh walked in. "Are you okay?" he asked Enid. He looked confused when he saw Mrs. Pratt.

"This is Andy Pratt's wife, Bernadette," Enid said.

"Nice to meet you." He glanced at Enid and then back to Bernadette. "I've got a SLED officer here with me. They're looking for Andy, so if you know where he is, you need to tell us."

"Andy has left the country, perhaps to Brazil," Enid said. "Bernadette overheard him planning to kill Abigail Sullivan."

Josh exhaled. "Whoa. I think I need to get SLED in here." He looked at Bernadette. "Miller Blakeley is dead. Do you know anything about that?"

"All I know is Andy's boss was upset that things were getting out of control. And they didn't trust Miller because of his drug dependency. Andy packed his bags earlier today and said he'd send for us later."

"Does he wear Italian loafers?"

"Excuse me?" Bernadette asked.

"Shoes, what kind did he have on today?"

"He almost always wears a pair of black Santoni loafers."

"I'm not familiar with that brand. I'm sure it's out of my price range," Josh said.

"It's an Italian brand," Mrs. Pratt said.

"Sit tight, both of you," Josh said.

He returned in a few minutes with SLED Officer Goodwin. "This is Andy Pratt's wife, Bernadette. I think you'll want to hear what she has to say."

Mrs. Pratt repeated what she had told Enid and Josh.

"Do you have the address of the house in Brazil?" Goodwin asked.

"No, but I know it's in Rio de Janeiro. Andy did some work there."

"It's a dangerous city for outsiders. Lots of crime. Was Andy connected to the drug scene there?"

Mrs. Pratt's shoulders slumped. "I know you think I'm one of those dumb, naive wives, and perhaps I am. But not long after we were married, I realized asking questions was dangerous. So I stopped. I tried to create a normal life for my son, to insulate both of us from Andy's business dealings."

"I'm not here to judge you, Mrs. Pratt. Just trying to understand the situation. Tell me about Mr. Adams, Andy's boss."

"I've never met him. I just know his name. He sent us to Blakeley to set up an agency because Andy said Mr. Adams told him it was fertile ground with only a small-town cop who wouldn't be a problem." She looked at Josh. "No offense, and you weren't here at the time."

"None taken," Josh said. "By fertile, was he referring to opportunities to deal drugs?"

Mrs. Pratt nodded. "I think they used Blakeley as a hub, you know, moving drugs in and out from here. I don't think they sold them here."

"What about Miller Blakeley?" Josh asked. "What was his relationship with Andy?"

"I don't know a lot about Mr. Blakeley, but Andy said he became addicted to oxycodone after some kind of surgery. Andy called him a 'desperate fool' but said he might come in handy because of his connections. And Blakeley offered his landing strip to Andy. I got the impression Miller was in a lot of debt and needed the money. Andy was concerned about Mrs. Blakeley, that she was going to turn them in."

"When Guinette Blakeley allegedly committed suicide, did you suspect Andy was involved?"

Mrs. Pratt's eyes filled with tears. "I know what it's like to be in a relationship with someone you're afraid of and who you know is doing something wrong. I've felt suicidal myself at times, but I wouldn't leave my son alone in this world. I thought perhaps she just became overwhelmed with the situation." She dabbed at her eyes. "Perhaps I didn't want to think of the alternative."

Enid took Mrs. Pratt's hand. "No one here blames you for being afraid and for protecting your son." Enid glanced at Josh and then at Officer Goodwin to underscore her comment.

Officer Goodwin was the first to respond. "I'm sure it

was a living hell for you, and I'm sorry for your situation."
He cleared his throat. "Did you have any knowledge that
Andy was going to kill Miller today?"

Mrs. Pratt sat up straight. "What?" She put her face in
her hands and sobbed. "I had no idea."

"I'm going to put you and your son in a safe place in
Columbia. And we'll need to get a formal statement from
you." He looked at Josh. "I need to put out an APB on Andy
and get Interpol involved." He turned to Josh. "Can you
handle things here until I can get back?"

"Sure, no problem."

The dispatcher tapped on the open door. "Chief Hart,
I'm sorry to bother you, but the mayor needs to see you right
away. At her place. And the governor wants an update asap."
She smiled as she walked away.

Officer Goodwin chuckled. "Ah, the joys of small-town
politics. Me, I'd rather deal with anyone other than a pissed
off, small-town mayor."

CHAPTER 50

The mayor of Blakeley had a small office next to the volunteer fire department but she rarely used it, instead preferring to hold meetings at her home. As a descendant of one of the town's founders, the mayor believed Blakeley could eventually return to its days of glory as a literary haven and fought hard to preserve that vision—or the illusion.

Amazingly, Josh had limited dealings with the mayor, especially since she was technically his boss. She had mostly left him alone. But after Guinette's death, she had appeared nervous and on edge, to the point that Josh often wondered about her relationship with the Blakeley family.

The mayor's house, like Miller's, was built when the town was founded and was often referred to as a money pit by the locals. The upkeep was horrendous on the beautiful old homes. Josh had no idea where she got her money, but it wasn't from being a part-time mayor in a small town like Blakeley.

When Josh arrived, the mayor was waiting for him in the formal living room. "Mayor, I understand you wanted to see me."

"Please call me Sylvia. Today just doesn't feel like a day for formalities. Would you like coffee?"

"That would be great, thanks."

An older woman appeared as if on cue, with a tray in hand. She set it on the table in front of the sofa and poured a cup for Josh. "Black, as I recall."

Impressed, Josh smiled. "Yes, thanks."

When the woman left the room, Sylvia wasted no time. "Who killed Miller?"

"We're still investigating."

"Don't assume that I'm stupid, Josh. May I call you that?" Without waiting for a reply, she continued. "But let me rephrase the question. Who do *you think* killed him?"

Josh was uncomfortable sharing information with her, but as mayor she had a right to know. "Indications are that Andy Pratt was involved. I can't say for sure if he pulled the trigger." He studied Sylvia's face for a reaction but saw none.

"Have you caught him?"

"No, ma'am. He filed a flight plan for Atlanta and there's a possibility he is headed out of the country."

Sylvia leaned her head back in the over-stuffed, uphol-stered chair. "That son of a bitch. I knew something was up with him."

"Why is that?"

"Guinette and I were friends, close friends. I was shocked when I heard she had committed suicide, but I also knew how depressed she was. And how upset she was with Miller. She was certain he and Andy were into illegal activi-ties, and she demanded that Miller end all contact with him. She hated her life here but felt compelled to keep up appear-ances, for the town's sake. After all, the Blakeleys are *the* family in this town. She felt trapped in the lies she was hav-ing to tell to protect Miller." Sylvia smiled slightly. "You know, in spite of everything, she loved him up until the end." She sighed. "But now, I see I should have sensed the danger she was in. I'll have to live with that."

"With all due respect, ma'am, why didn't you tell me all this sooner?"

"Because I knew you were here on assignment for Larkin. And I didn't want him to call in SLED and rip this town apart."

"I'm sorry I didn't earn your trust so that you could have confided in me."

Sylvia shrugged. "Not your fault. Not at all. Blakeley is a small, incestuous bed of secrets and sin."

"Someone else characterized the town in the same way."

"I was also friends with Abigail Sullivan, and she used that phrase often. I thought she was being overly dramatic and told her that was a good title for a novel. I hardly thought it described our sleepy little town." She held up both hands, as if surrendering. "But of course, she was right." She stared intently at Josh. "I suppose Abigail's death will be reopened now too."

"Yes, ma'am. I imagine it will."

"Poor Timmy. I hope you find a good home for him. I'm not the motherly type myself or I'd offer."

"Abigail asked Petula Grant to take care of Timmy if anything happened. Now Petula's cousin is filing for guardianship. She and Timmy hit it off instantly."

"Oh, that's wonderful. I'm so glad."

The woman who had brought the coffee in appeared at the door. "I'm sorry to disturb you, but Governor Larkin is on the phone and would like to talk with Chief Hart." She paused. "He said it was urgent." She turned to Josh. "You can take the call in the study. It's private."

When she left, Josh stood but paused before following her. "Will Blakeley be able to survive all this?"

"This town has weathered a lot, but I'm not sure this time. Even though most of us know the Blakeleys are not saints, this is a lot to take in, especially for some of our founding families." The mayor appeared to be gathering her thoughts. "And we'll need to talk more about your future here when all this is behind us."

As Josh walked down the long hall to the study, her words echoed in his head. Maybe that was her subtle way of preparing him to be fired.

CHAPTER 51

After Josh gave Governor Larkin all the information he had, he waited for Larkin's reaction, not sure what to expect.

"Could we have prevented Miller's murder if we had moved quicker?" Larkin asked.

Josh chose his words carefully. "Sir, this killing is a tragedy, but we must also remember that Miller was likely involved in drug trafficking, insurance fraud, and possibly even murder. He's not an innocent victim."

"We need to be careful about accusing the head of the founding family until we have proof. Do you have that kind of proof?"

"No, sir, but I'm sure we can make a case against Miller with SLED's support." Josh again paused to consider his words. "To be honest, I'm surprised at how many people in this town suspected Miller was involved in illegal activities but said nothing to me. I guess I really am an outsider here, even more than I assumed."

"Well, that's unfortunate. So where do we go from here?"

With your permission, I'd like to work with SLED to reopen the Guinette Blakeley and Abigail Sullivan cases. I think they're both tied to Miller Blakeley and Andy Pratt."

Larkin exhaled loudly, as though releasing something he had been holding onto for a long time. "I golfed with Miller. Our wives were friends. I can't get my head around him

232 · RAEGAN TELLER

being involved in drugs, murder, and who knows what else. But I'm not going to interfere in any way. The chips will just have to fall where they may. I'll ask SLED to include you on the investigation team."

"Thank you, sir. Oh, and there's one more thing I need." Josh explained Timmy's situation and Meredith's application for guardianship." I'm not asking the Department of Social Services to shortcut Meredith's background check. I want to be as sure as anyone that she's qualified to be a guardian. But I know these things can get bogged down in bureaucracy. So if there's anything you can do to keep the process moving along, the better off Timmy will be. He desperately needs stability and a good home."

"I can do that for the boy."

"Thank you."

"After the investigation is wrapped up, let's sit down and talk. I assume you're not interested in staying in Blakeley, and I can't blame you. You are certainly overqualified for the position."

"I appreciate that sir, but I'm going to let Enid decide our next move. She gave up a lot for me. This time, I want her to do what she wants to do, even if it means I have to give up law enforcement."

"That would be a shame, given your experience and knowledge. But it's admirable. Still, let's talk to see if we can figure out a win-win for you and Ingrid."

"It's Enid, sir. Her name is Enid."

"Yes, of course. Wait, hold just a minute."

Josh tried to push the overwhelming uncertainty of his future from his mind while waiting for Larkin to return. Josh knew he wasn't good at operating in limbo, and it seems that's where he had been the past few years. Timmy wasn't the only one that needed stability.

"I'm back," Larkin said. "Sorry for the interruption. I just got word that Andy Pratt was apprehended at the Hartsfield-Jackson Atlanta International Airport. He was waiting to board a flight to Brazil. He's being transported to Columbia for questioning."

CHAPTER 52

After Pratt's arrest, he demanded to talk to his attorney, who was flying in from Chicago. The next day, Officer Goodwin was contacted by Pratt's attorney, who wanted to cut a deal by giving them information about the drug network in exchange for a reduced sentence. Without making promises, SLED agent Goodwin told him they would consider anything Pratt gave them that helped with the investigation.

When the attorney informed Goodwin that Pratt was ready to talk, they proceeded to take his statement under oath.

Five hours later, Pratt had given them a plethora of names of those he claimed were the "real guilty ones." When Pratt implicated his boss Nathan Adams as the kingpin of the entire operation, SLED immediately ran a check on him but nothing came back. Pratt's response was, "He's not stupid enough to use his real name." Pratt claimed he didn't know what it was, so the FBI was called in since the crimes involved interstate trafficking.

Pratt also implicated Miller Blakeley and claimed he was called to Miller's house, and then Miller tried to kill him. No one in the interrogation room believed Miller's killing was self-defense, and Pratt had nothing on his phone or any proof he had been summoned by Miller.

When asked about Dr. Edwards, the local dentist who freely prescribed Oxy to Miller, Pratt replied that Edwards was just another useful idiot. Pratt denied Edwards being a part of their operations, although Goodwin made a note to investigate him further.

When Pratt was asked about Guinette Blakeley, he initially refused to answer. Goodwin reminded Pratt's attorney that if Pratt wanted a reduced sentence, he would have to cooperate. "Did you split the insurance proceeds with Miller Blakeley?" Goodwin asked.

Pratt's attorney responded, "If they did, hypothetically speaking of course, it wasn't Andy's idea. You need to look at Miller Blakeley's financial situation. He was drowning in debt."

"Was the coroner involved? Did you pay him off to say her death was suicide?"

Pratt looked down at the table.

"We're going to have the body exhumed, so I'm only asking to give you a chance to earn some good-boy points with me. I don't care if you answer or not."

Pratt nodded.

"What does that mean?" Goodwin asked. "Are you confirming the coroner was involved?"

"Miller just asked him, as an old friend, to hurry up the report. Nothing else."

"What about Abigail Sullivan?" Goodwin asked. "Did you *arrange* for her to fall down the stairs?"

Pratt's attorney shook his head and his client responded, "No comment."

"What about Petula Grant, the thrift shop owner?"

Pratt looked at his attorney, who nodded, and then said. "I had nothing to do with that. Miller wanted to find out what she had from Abigail."

Tired and disgusted by Pratt's games, Goodwin pounded his fist on the table. "Let me tell you one thing, you piece of shit, you've left a trail of broken lives behind you. If you ever want to see daylight again, you'd better start telling me the truth. A little boy's life was upended, and the woman who took him in is dead now too. Now either start talking or I'll make sure you get the maximum sentence possible." He hit the table again. "Got that?"

The attorney whispered something in Pratt's ear and then replied. "I think he's said enough."

"One last question. Who owns the house in Brazil? You or someone else?"

The attorney nodded, and Pratt replied, "As a sales bonus, I was given unlimited use of the house."

"Why Brazil? Did your drug enterprise have connections there?"

"That's where I met Nate Adams. He went by the name Jose Santos and offered me a job."

Goodwin chuckled. "Likely not his real name. Santos in Brazil is like Smith or Jones. But we'll check it out."

Goodwin shoved a pad and pen toward Pratt. "Write down the exact location of the house, any phone numbers or addresses you have for your boss, and anything else that you'd better pray is helpful."

CHAPTER 53

Enid and Timmy were next door at Pet's apartment, gathering Timmy's belongings. "Why are we packing up my things? Am I going to live with Miss Meredith?"

Enid sat on the small single bed and motioned for Timmy to sit down also. "Remember, we told you that you don't have to go anywhere you don't want to. But we have to get your things out of here because someone wants to buy the shop." She pulled Timmy closer and squeezed his shoulders gently. "Where do you want to live?"

"I like you and Josh, and I like Miss Meredith. But . . ." His soft voice trailed off.

"Timmy, if you want to go live with Miss Meredith, Josh and I will come to see you. And you can visit us." She added, "Once we get settled somewhere."

His face lit up. "You'll come see me? Really?"

"I promise. But you understand, she has to wait for approval, so you might have to stay with us until that happens."

"That's okay."

"By the way, has your grandmother come to visit you again? I haven't heard you mention her."

Timmy shook his head. "I asked her to come see me, but she hasn't."

"Maybe she knows you're safe and have a good home

waiting for you. She'll always be there for you, even if you don't see her."

"I know."

"So let's finish packing these things."

. . .

By the time Enid and Timmy got back to the shop, Josh was home. "I thought maybe you had both run away."

"We were next door, packing." She opened the storage room door and said to Timmy, "We can put your things in here for now. Unless you want them upstairs in your room."

Timmy nodded. "We can put them here."

Josh made eye contact with Enid and then said to Timmy, "Why don't you go upstairs and let us talk for a few minutes? Then we'll rustle up some food. I don't know about you, but I'm hungry."

"Me too," Timmy said as he ran up the stairs.

Josh filled Enid in on what was happening with the case. "So are you still involved?" Enid asked.

"As much as I want to be. But SLED has everything under control. Oh, and I met with the mayor too. She and the governor both hinted I might soon be unemployed."

Enid laughed. "Looks like I married a man who can't hold onto a job."

"Ouch. That hurts." Josh looked around the shop. "If you want, we can buy another shop wherever we go." He paused. "But this move will be your choice. You followed me here, and you've done a great job trying to make this a home for us. So you tell me, when you're ready, where we're going next."

Enid picked up one of the books on the table. "I love this shop. But I don't love running it." She kissed him on the cheek. "I love you for giving me the choice, but it will be *our* choice, not just mine. I've decided to do some free-lance writing and reporting, but I can do that from anywhere."

"Miller's family envisioned this town would encourage writers, so I guess it worked, on you at least. I just want you to be happy. Understand?"

Enid nodded. "What about Timmy?"

"Oh, I almost forgot. Governor Larkin had that private investigator, the one I met with who does work for him, he had her do a thorough background check on Meredith. The woman is a saint, or close to it. She's highly respected in the education community and for her work with local charities. So he's talked with the head of DSS, explained Timmy's situation, and requested they expedite Meredith's request for guardianship."

"It certainly helps to know the right people. Thanks for doing that."

"Do you hate to see him go?"

Enid smiled. "He's a great kid. But being a mother takes a lot of time and energy. And I'm so happy Meredith wants to take him. They're perfect together. And she's already found someone who will buy the shop's contents, assume the lease, and continue running it."

"Based on the background check, Meredith is in good financial shape, but Will and Nellie will appreciate having the funds to maintain the farm."

Josh stood up. "Now let's find something to eat."

CHAPTER 54

A few weeks later, Josh was surprised to get a call from Tiffany, the private investigator. He agreed to drive to Columbia for coffee at her office.

When he arrived, she showed him to her small conference room. "Is that one of those Nespresso machines I've seen advertised?" he asked.

"It is. Would you like an espresso or regular coffee?"

Josh smiled. "Just plain old coffee. I tried an espresso once and didn't sleep for two nights."

Tiffany laughed. "You get used to it. There are times when I have to stay awake and need the extra jolt. But such is the life of a PI."

Josh looked around the room. "Doesn't look like a bad life. The few PIs I know can't pay the rent."

"It helps to have the right clients."

"By the way, Governor Larkin said you did a thorough background check on Meredith. Thanks for getting that done so quickly. I'd love to see Timmy settled in somewhere soon."

Tiffany laughed. "Tired of fatherhood?"

"Let's just say it's all working out for the best."

"What will you do now? Surely you don't plan to stay in Blakeley."

"That seems to be the popular consensus, that we're leaving."

"You know, Columbia is a nice place. It still has a bit of a small-town atmosphere, but it's big enough to make it interesting and fun."

"Are you trying to sell me on Columbia?"

Meredith pulled a folder from the credenza and slid it across the table to Josh. "Don't be mad, but I ran a background check on you. You have quite a history. Undercover narcotics work, homicide detective, police chief, sheriff."

Josh ignored the folder. "Who asked you to run the check? Or can you tell me?"

"Someone who wants to offer you a job."

"I'm not ready to take a job. As I told Larkin, Enid gets to decide the next move."

"That's so admirable of you."

Josh stood to leave. "Is there anything else you needed to talk to me about?"

Tiffany motioned for him to sit back down. "Don't sulk. Please. I want to offer you a job."

Josh remained standing. "A job? Working for you? Doing what? I have no desire to follow married men around to catch them cheating."

Tiffany laughed again. "I don't do that kind of work. Most of my assignments are to check out people, often people in high places. This is the capital city, you know. Lots of government work. I help vet people who are being considered for certain positions, or someone from either political party who might want to run for an office. It pays well, good hours, and you get to attend a lot of great parties."

"In case you didn't find out in your background check, I'm not a party kind of guy. A cold beer or a glass of wine now and then is about as wild as I get."

"Fair enough. I'll take care of the parties. And I know you've got to run this past Enid. I'd like to meet her and have her meet me. I can connect her with the right people." She motioned to Josh's chair again. "Please sit and let's talk details."

CHAPTER 55

Nearly a month later, Enid walked into Tiffany's office. Enid had resisted meeting with her, but when Tiffany insisted it would be worth her time, Enid agreed to a short visit.

When Josh learned of the meeting, he warned Enid that Tiffany was a bit stubborn, much like her, which didn't go over well. He had decided if the two women didn't hit it off, there was no way he was taking the job. Not that he had decided anyway. He still had reservations about doing background checks. He was a law enforcement guy, not a report writer. But he promised he would keep an open mind. The mayor of Blakeley had told him he could stay in the police chief position if he wanted to, but also suggested he might be happier elsewhere.

As Josh anticipated, Miller's fall from grace had not gone over well with Blakeley's citizens, especially the ones whose relatives had founded the town. Some even blamed Josh for stirring up the trouble that got Miller killed. The mayor suggested the town might dismantle the Blakeley Police Department and instead rely on the county sheriff's protection. Josh felt fired, even though those words were never spoken. When he shared this information with Enid, she agreed to meet with Tiffany.

"Thank you for meeting with me," Tiffany said to Enid. "I've heard so much about you that I feel like I know you."

"I'm here for Josh's sake."

"Right. No girl talk. I get it. So, here's the deal. He'll work for me initially. If things work out, we can consider making him a partner. I imagine he's already discussed the salary I offered."

"It's very generous. More than he's made since he left New Mexico. But we live a simple life, so money is not the primary motivator for us."

"No, I get that. But I read your news stories, which were quite impressive. You've said on several occasions you wanted to get to the truth, that's why you became a journalist."

"That's true. But what's that got to do with Josh?"

"Because my work is about finding the truth too. It's about making sure people are who they say they are. A lot depends on finding the right people for these positions. Sometimes I have to turn down some work because I think a man is needed to do the investigation. I won't lie to you. Some of the work is undercover, and Josh's experience will be invaluable. I tried out a few guys that just didn't work out, but I believe Josh would be a good fit."

"But I don't know if Josh would be happy doing that kind of work."

"I'd like for both of you to give me a chance, give the job and Columbia a chance." Tiffany handed a paper containing a typed list to Enid. "These people are interested in having you do freelance reporting or writing for them, since you said you wanted to remain independent for now. I didn't have to look far, and I could double that list. You're well respected, especially for a reporter from a weekly rag."

Enid took the paper and skimmed it. "This is an impressive list. Thank you."

"And I just want to get one thing straight with you. I may kid around and even flirt at times. It's part of my shtick, you might say. Comes in handy in my line of work. But I'm strictly business. I admire Josh's experience and knowledge. He likes to dig for answers, and that's what I need. That and someone I can trust. And you can trust me to do what's right for Josh. For both of you."

Enid smiled for the first time. "Thanks for your honesty. Josh is the most honest and trustworthy man I've ever known."

"He told me he was leaving the next move up to you. I'm sorry things didn't work out in Blakeley."

"Don't be. We both knew it was temporary."

"If he wants to try out this gig, I'll help you find a good rental. Living downtown is great, but if you prefer the suburbs, I know several good agents who can find you a house with a yard and all the trimmings. You can rent until you're sure this is right—for both of you."

Enid stood. "I'm glad I met with you. Josh will be back in touch since it's ultimately his decision."

CHAPTER 56

Several weeks later, Josh walked down the stairs from the apartment into the bookstore and saw Timmy sitting in one of the chairs looking at a book. Several suitcases were sitting nearby. The fat arms of the huge stuffed chair embraced the small boy as if trying to protect him from the cruel world.

"Hey, buddy, what you reading?"

Timmy held up the book for Josh to see. "This is the coolest book on ghosts." A big grin engulfed his face.

"Maybe you shouldn't be reading scary stuff like that. Might keep you awake."

Timmy's grin faded. "I wanna see Nana again. Maybe I can learn how to make her come back to see me."

Josh kneeled down beside Timmy's chair. "I've got something I want to give you. It's like a book, written by your grandmother."

"Nana wrote it?"

Josh nodded. "She wanted you to have it when you were older. But I think you're old enough now to understand. You've had to grow up pretty fast." Josh tousled Timmy's sandy brown hair.

Timmy nodded.

Josh walked over to the antique desk where Enid handled all the sales transactions and picked up the worn leather-bound journal. The faded initials AS were embossed in the bottom corner of the cover. He handed the book to Timmy.

"Here you go, buddy. If there's anything you want to talk about after reading this, just let me know. Your grandmother was a brave woman."

Josh sat down in the other reading chair beside him. "I want you to know that if you ever need to talk to me, you can call me anytime. Okay?"

Timmy nodded and then jumped up and threw his arms around Josh's neck. "Thank you."

"You're welcome, buddy. We're going to miss you, but I know you'll be happy with Meredith."

"We're going to get a horse."

"That's great, buddy. I'm happy for you. And when you get settled, we'll take you to visit our friend Jack in Madden."

The bell hanging on the door sounded, and Meredith walked in. "Hi, Josh. Timmy, are you ready to go?"

"Yes, ma'am."

Meredith held out her hand to Josh. "I can't thank you enough for all you and Enid have done."

"Where is Enid?" Timmy asked.

Enid called from the top of the stairs. I'm headed down right now." She appeared with a plastic container. "These are goodies from Tess. She said she'll miss you." She handed the container to Meredith. "I'll miss both of you, but we'll come to visit soon."

Timmy hugged Enid. "I love you."

Enid fought back tears. "I love you too, little man. If I had a son, I would want him to be just like you."

"Are you closing this store?"

"Only for a little while. The new owner will take over in a few weeks."

Meredith hugged Enid. "I guess we'd better get on the road. We'll see you again soon." She turned to Josh. "And congratulations on the new job. Sounds exciting."

"I hope it's pretty dull, actually. I've had enough excitement to last for a while. But thanks."

"Columbia is a nice city. I think you'll be happy there."

"Thanks. I'll help you get these things to the car."

Josh put Timmy's suitcases in Meredith's SUV and returned inside. "Well, I guess we're alone again," he said to Enid. His cell phone rang. Officer Goodwin's number appeared on his screen. "Hey, what's up?" Josh said.

"Just wanted to let you know we arrested Nate Adams, aka Jose Santos, which was also a fake name, as we figured. He's being extradited back to the US. Apparently, Interpol is interested in him too for international drug smuggling, as well as a few unsolved murders. Who'd imagine an insurance executive would turn out to be the bad guy."

"Thanks for the update. I guess you know I've resigned the police chief position."

"Heard you were going to work for Tiffany. She's quite a character."

"You know her?"

Goodwin laughed. "Oh, yeah. But she's good people. I think you'll like working with her. And by the way, the coroner confessed to taking a payoff to sign off on Guinette Blakeley's autopsy. Says he had no idea what had happened, and thought it was suicide just like Miller said. We got a court order to exhume the body since there are no immediate relatives to give consent. But it likely won't show anything other than a drug overdose, which we already know. But we have to be sure." He made eye contact with Josh. "And in case you're having any doubts about your investigation for Governor Larkin, Pratt was careful to use the town of Blakeley as his base of operations but didn't conduct illegal drug activities there, other than using Miller's landing strip to transport goods."

"Thanks, I appreciate you saying that. So I guess Andy Pratt will go down for Guinette's death as well as Miller's."

"The state prosecutor has agreed to take the death penalty off the table for Guinette Miller's murder in exchange for Pratt's cooperation. His wife is also going to testify against him, so we've got a good case. But he's likely going away for life."

"What about Abigail Sullivan?"

Goodwin sighed. "I wish for the boy's sake I could give you good news. But Pratt knows we can't prove she didn't fall accidentally, and so far he's not admitting to helping her down those stairs. He denies that conversation with his boss his wife claims to have overheard. A sad situation."

"And Petula Grant?"

"Pratt still insists that was Miller Blakeley's doing. Pratt said Miller was trying to find whatever documentation Abigail might have given her that would incriminate Miller. We may never be able to solve that one."

"That's too bad, but I appreciate the update."

"If you ever miss law enforcement and want to come to SLED, just let me know."

"Thanks, I will. But I'm looking forward to seeing how the other side lives, you know, the people who don't have a target on them all the time. And Enid is excited about her new contract work with the *State* newspaper. And she's also writing a book about Blakeley. Since I'm no longer the police chief, the governor gave her the green light. Of course, he'll have to approve it before publication. Can't embarrass the governor, now can we."

Goodwin laughed. "Politics. Gotta love it. Well, keep in touch and best of luck to you and Enid."

CHAPTER 57

As Enid watched the movers put the last boxes on the truck, a red pickup drove up and parked on the street. "Roo, what a pleasant surprise. I didn't know you were in town."

"I'm meeting with SLED this afternoon on Guinette's case. But I wanted to say goodbye."

"We're just going to Columbia. Once we're settled into our new place, you can visit. We'll always have a spare bedroom for you."

Josh walked out to join them. "Hey, Roo." He hugged her. "I guess you know all the bad guys have been caught. And it was you who triggered the investigation. You should feel good about the way it turned out."

"Yeah, I do. I mean, it's hard to feel good when so many people died. But the good news is I hear you're working for Tiffany now," she said grinning.

"Yes, and as a matter of fact, I'm looking for an assistant. I already have more than I can manage, and I haven't even started yet. Know anyone who might be interested?" He pointed to Roo.

"Are you serious? For real?"

Josh and Enid laughed. "He was going to call you soon and see if you might like to work for him," Enid said.

"OMG, yes! Of course. We're going to have so much fun." She paused. "You're not joking, are you?"

Josh put his arm around her. "No. Call me tomorrow and

let's talk about the details."

"I will." Roo glanced at the time on her phone. "I gotta run. And thank you." She jogged to her pickup.

"I think you made her happy," Enid said.

"Yeah, but now I've got to put up with you, Tiffany, and Roo. I'm not sure I can handle that many strong women. Whatever happened to the good old days when women were subservient?"

Enid faked a punch to his stomach. "You're such a bad liar." She took his hand and led him into the shop. "Help me look around and make sure we've got everything."

Inside the shop, Josh surveyed the place. "Despite everything that's happened, I have some good memories of Blakeley."

"Me too." Enid squeezed his hand. "But I'm ready to make some new memories. I've had enough sin and secrets to last me a lifetime."

PLEASE...
A humble request from the author

Thank you for taking time from your busy schedule to read this (or any other) book. The world needs more readers like you.

I hope you enjoyed *Murder Clause*. If so, please do me a big favor and leave a review on Amazon and/or Goodreads. Reviews encourage other readers to explore authors with whom they may not be familiar.

Thank you in advance for taking the time to do a review!

www.Amazon.com

www.Goodreads.com

• • •

If you'd like to contact me directly, please visit my website: www.RaeganTeller.com/contact. I'd love to hear from you.

AUTHOR NOTES

Inspiration for my novels often comes from the news headlines. I am always on the lookout for stories that ignite my imagination, especially those that deal with family tragedies or unusual circumstances.

When I began looking for the inspiration for this sixth novel, I didn't have to look far. The chilling events surrounding the Alex Murdaugh case left an indelible mark not only on South Carolina but on the entire nation—and on my imagination.

Sometimes, it's not enough to have imagination—you need motivation as well, and I have my muses to motivate me. For me, the victims of real crimes, like those in the Murdaugh case, are my muses, my motivation to keep writing.

Since my stories typically deal with the aftermath of a crime and its effects on the families involved, this case was fertile ground. One Murdaugh victim in particular, Gloria Satterfield, tugged at my psyche. Allegedly, she fell down the stairs and died. But to add to the family's misfortune, Alex Murdaugh stole the life insurance money that was intended for her family, one of whom was a handicapped son.

Whether or not Murdaugh had anything to do with Satterfield's death has not been established. But he certainly committed a cruel crime against the Satterfield family. As an author, I felt compelled to explore this theme. Through the pages of *Murder Clause*, I fabricated a tale that delves into the complexities of human nature, the darkness that can lurk beneath the surface, and the pursuit of truth and justice.

But as I was writing, another theme emerged. In the Preface, I talked about Enid's search for her own truth, which became another dominant theme of the story. Finding the balance between life and career is a challenge, one I confronted throughout my own career.

As you turned the pages of *Murder Clause,* I hope you found yourself captivated by the characters and their stories, and that you were reminded of the importance of seeking your own truth—even when the answers remain elusive.

Will this be the last book in the series? I honestly don't know. I've predicted the end several times, but Enid keeps pulling me back into her life. So, we'll see what happens.

ACKNOWLEDGMENTS

First and foremost, I must express my deepest gratitude to my rock, my anchor, my ever-supportive husband, Earl. Without him, this novel would have remained just another unsolved mystery. As my "roadie" (as he describes himself), Earl has been by my side, managing our book orders, helping me schedule events, and setting up displays. He also works tirelessly to keep our household running smoothly while I'm hiding away writing. Through all the twists and turns of this journey, he has kept me sane. Earl, for all this and more, I can never thank you enough.

To my wonderful sister Jane, to my friends, and to all the amazing people who have endured my hectic schedule, your understanding and encouragement have been a beacon of light in the darkest of moments. I am truly blessed to have each of you in my life.

A special note of gratitude goes to Irene Stern, the brilliant Novel Mechanic, who has meticulously edited, proofed, and formatted this book. Irene, your keen eye and expertise have been invaluable. And our friendship is a treasure I cherish. Perhaps most importantly, according to Eli and Katrina, you are the "best pet sitter ever." What would we all do without you?

Last, but certainly not least, I want to extend my heartfelt thanks to my incredible readers. Your unwavering loyalty has been the fuel that drives me to continue writing, even when I feel like giving up. You are the reason I strive to create mysteries that keep you guessing. I am forever grateful for your passion for my stories and your enthusiasm for my characters. Thank you all, from the bottom of my heart.

ABOUT THE AUTHOR

Raegan Teller is the award-winning author of the Enid Blackwell mysteries. Her debut novel was *Murder in Madden*, followed by five additional volumes in the series. Two of her novels earned Honorable Mentions in the Writer's Digest Self-Published Book Awards, receiving judges' comments like "exemplary in its structure, organization, and pacing," "one of the best I've read this year," "great job combining the plot and character," and "great storyteller." Set in and around her hometown of Columbia, Teller's mysteries delve into small-town intrigue, family secrets, and murderous plots. Although her books are fictional, each is inspired by a real-life event.

A summa cum laude graduate of Queens University, Charlotte, Teller is an active member of several writing organizations, including Sisters in Crime, South Carolina Writers Association, Women's Fiction Writers Association, Charlotte Writers Club, and ALLi (Alliance of Independent Authors). To learn more about Raegan Teller and her work, visit https://RaeganTeller.com

Made in the USA
Middletown, DE
23 September 2023

38725204R00161